NOV 15

THE PEDDLER'S ROAD

THE PEDDLER'S ROAD

THE SECRETS OF THE PIED PIPER

BOOK I

Matthew Cody

ALFRED A. KNOPF
NEW YORK

THIS IS A BORZOI BOOK PUBLISHED BY ALFRED A. KNOPF

Text copyright © 2015 by Matthew Cody
Jacket art and interior illustrations copyright © 2015 by Craig Phillips

Visit us on the Web! randomhousekids.com

Educators and librarians, for a variety of teaching tools, visit us at RHTeachersLibrarians.com

Library of Congress Cataloging-in-Publication Data
Cody, Matthew.
The Peddler's road / Matthew Cody.—First edition.
p. cm.—(The secrets of the Pied Piper ; 1)
Summary: While in Germany with their father, who is researching the Pied Piper legend, Max, nearly thirteen, and her brother Carter, ten, are spirited away to the magical land where the stolen children of Hamelin have been hidden since the thirteenth century.
ISBN 978-0-385-75522-1 (trade)—ISBN 978-0-385-75523-8 (lib. bdg.)—
ISBN 978-0-385-75524-5 (ebook)
[1. Pied Piper of Hamelin (Legendary character)—Fiction. 2. Magic—Fiction.
3. Brothers and sisters—Fiction. 4. Fantasy.] I. Title.
PZ7.C654Ped 2015
[Fic]—dc23
2014041130

The text of this book is set in 12-point Requiem.

Printed in the United States of America
October 2015
10 9 8 7 6 5 4 3 2 1

First Edition

This one's all for Willem.

This wall was built in 1556,
272 years after the magician stole 130
children away.

—Inscription found on the old town
wall in Hamelin, Germany

In the old days at home the Neverland
had always begun to look a little dark and
threatening by bedtime. Then unexplored
patches arose in it and spread; black shadows
moved about in them; the roar of the beasts
of prey was quite different now, and above
all, you lost the certainty that you could win.

—J. M. Barrie,
Peter Pan and Wendy

*I*t's been four days since the other children left me behind. Father Warner asked me if I would write down exactly what happened. Being a learned boy, I should put my tale to parchment. Memory becomes slippery with age, he said, and someday someone might want to know. They might need to know, lest it ever happen again.

The men of the village returned this evening in despair. They followed the trail as far as the mountain, but there it stopped. That many feet leave obvious tracks, and yet the footprints disappeared when they reached the base of the mountain. It has been decided that tomorrow the men will use nets to scour the river Weser for bodies, but they will not find any. The children are gone, but they are not dead.

Grandmother says all we can do now is pray, and that I must stay inside tonight, and tomorrow, too. People are overcome with grief, and if they see that I am still here, they will not understand why only one hundred thirty children were taken—why not one hundred thirty-one? Every other child over the age of three was lost, so why not me? Why spare a lame boy but not their own sons and daughters? What good am I, anyway, with my crutch and my twisted, useless leg—and why are their healthy, strong boys gone, their beautiful daughters vanished?

People in this state can be dangerous, Grandmother says, even friends and neighbors. She tells a story of when her own mother was just a little girl and the winter was hard and food was scarce, how the townsfolk drove a poor woman and her child out into the snow because they suspected the child's mother of witchcraft. It is still whispered by some that the woman cursed the village that night and that the rats appeared the very next day. Father Warner says such stories are foolish, but he agrees with Grandmother that even foolish people can do terrible things when they are scared or angry.

Therefore, I sit in my room and do as the priest asks of me, and write by candlelight while the church bells ring in the square. Grandmother always says they ring for the poor souls wandering in Purgatory, but tonight I think they ring for the living.

I think the rest of the children would have left me, but Lukas was always uncommonly kind. It was he who knocked on my window on the night after the Piper drove the rats from our village. There wasn't a child alive in Hamelin who hadn't been bitten in the crib, and the creatures haunted our dreams. When the other boys my age were going out to take their revenge by throwing stones at the rats in the alleyways, Lukas would sometimes invite me along. But I did not like the names the other children called me, and I did not like the sounds the rats made when the stones hit. I would tell him my leg hurt too much, or that I had to work in Father's shop. "Tomorrow," I promised. Always tomorrow. Lukas never argued. "Tomorrow, then," he would say, and that was that.

I suppose that was why, when I woke up to find him tapping on my window shutter, I was not afraid, even though I could not imagine what he would be doing there at that time of night, with the moon so high in the sky. "Listen, Timm," he whispered through the shutter cracks. "Can you hear it?"

At first I thought he might be walking in his sleep and that this was all part of a dream, but then I heard it, too. Far away still, but clear as a prayer bell. I think by that time the Piper must have reached the north gate, where he had gathered most of the children. It was only the very small ones and the stragglers that were still missing.

It is hard to describe what that music sounded like, and I cannot reproduce the melody, though many have since asked me to try. The best I can do is to say that it made me sad. Unbearably so. It was a mournful piping without words, yet it spoke to me and told me how sorry it was for our place here, for our brief lives yet to come.

Lukas helped me through my window. He held my crutches as I climbed, and he caught me when I fell. Once outside, I saw that other shapes were moving in the dark. The few remaining children, desperate not to be left behind, ran toward the song. Lukas could have left me, but he did not. I hobbled along as best I could, and he kept pace with me as we answered the Piper's call.

I could not see the Piper clearly as we marched out of Hamelin. He was far away, at the head of the line, and all I saw was a glimpse of his hood and his motley coat in the moonlight, with its red, yellow and green patches sewn into it. But the music was stronger now. As we left the city walls and set out across the fields toward the mountain woods, the song in my head disappeared, and in its place a landscape filled my heart.

Sunlight. Green trees and sweet flowers. Fireflies in the shade. Honey dripping from the trees and warm summer air. Games and toadstools and magic. Real magic. A land older than time, where we would stay young forever. This was where we were going, and the farther we traveled from our homes, the less sad I felt. My despair began to lift, and I knew that I would soon be leaving all my cares and pains behind me.

I have not told Father Warner this, but it felt like the way he describes heaven.

Alas, in the end, I could not keep pace. My crutches lodged in the mud, and I tripped on a root hidden in the dark. Eventually, even the smallest children passed me by until the only one left was Lukas. The line was disappearing ahead of us, into a cave under the mountain. But they weren't walking into darkness; they were walking into sunlight. One by one they entered, and then the light began to fade. It dwindled until it looked like just a pinhole at the end of that long tunnel. The doorway to the promised land was closing, and my sadness returned. Heavy and heartbreaking.

I do not blame Lukas for running on ahead. If I could have dropped my crutches and run, I would have. I would have left him behind. I would have run even if my leg had snapped beneath me. Then I would have crawled. But by this point, even crawling was an agony. Lukas looked back at me once, I think, though I cannot be sure. Before long, he too disappeared into the mountain.

I lay there for a time, listening to the music getting softer and softer, until it finally faded to silence. Then, like a baby, I cried myself to sleep.

The townsfolk found me at sunrise, shivering in the mud. I told them what had happened, and at first they did not believe me. But the tracks were impossible to ignore, and so a search party made up of the men of our village set out to look for the missing children.

Four days of useless searching.

Father Warner tells me that I am blessed. That God in His wisdom made my leg this way so that I would be spared, so that I could stay behind and warn others of the Piper in the pied coat, and of the dangers of bargaining with such a man, if man he was.

There will be funerals, I suppose, although the children are not dead. I know this in my heart. We will mourn Lukas and all the rest, but I will not cry for them.

Like the rest of our village, I pray every night. But I do not pray for the children of Hamelin. I pray for me. I pray that the Piper will come back for me, and that I will be allowed to join the rest of the children in the place of sunlight. I dream about it every night.

I fear I will go mad with dreaming.

(From the journal of Timm Weaver, 1284)

PART I

HAMELIN

CHAPTER ONE

Once there was a girl called Max who had pink hair. According to the label on the dye bottle, the hair color was actually *Rosa,* which the nice lady at the pharmacy assured her translated to "Wild Magenta," but in the end it turned out to be ordinary pink. The whole process was far messier than Max had expected, and though she'd read that she'd need a second person to really do the job right, she'd decided to tackle it by herself. There wasn't anyone around to help her, anyway.

She'd imagined trying out pink hair would be like trying out a new Max. The Max that came in the Wild Magenta bottle would be impulsive and free-spirited and exactly the kind of girl who dyed her hair pink one morning on a whim. But as she stared morosely at the bathroom sink and at all the places the dye had stained the porcelain, she didn't feel any different at all. She was just . . . pinker.

As she examined her new look in the bathroom mirror (she'd accidentally dyed the tip of her left ear, too), her brother, Carter, was banging on the bathroom door, telling her he had to go.

"What could you possibly be doing in there that would take this long?" her brother complained from the other side of the door, and "If I have to break the door, we'll both be sorry, especially me, because the door looks really, really sturdy."

Max turned the lock and yanked the door open in one quick motion. She was so fast that Carter was left banging on nothing at all for a second or two before he realized that the door wasn't closed anymore.

Carter had just turned ten, and Max was nearly thirteen, so Max had a good four inches on her younger brother, even when she slouched (which was something she did a lot). She stared down at her brother as she waited for the inevitable snarky quip. There was no way Carter would pass up an opportunity to make fun of her new pink hair. Maybe he'd say she looked like one of those troll dolls you get out of those fifty-cent machines (Max worried that she kind of did). But Carter kept quiet as he shimmied by her, a pained look of concentration on his face as he squeezed his knees together.

As they passed each other, Max bumped into Carter and he stumbled on his bad leg, barely catching himself on the marble washbasin.

"Oh! Carter, I'm sorry!" said Max, but her brother waved her away.

"I'm fine," he said. "But can I have some privacy, for Pete's sake?"

Max stepped out into the hallway as her brother slammed the door shut. The squeaking floorboards beneath her feet made Max think of chewing on tinfoil. The floorboards back at their apartment in the States didn't creak like that. Their neighbor who smelled like mothballs let her alarm go off for hours in the morning, and you couldn't sleep at night with the windows open because of the sounds of people spilling out of the bar across the street, but at least the floorboards stayed quiet.

Carter called to her from behind the bathroom door. "You've turned your ear pink, you know," he said.

Little monster.

When Max went down to the kitchen, she found half a carafe of cold coffee on the table and the lingering, apple-y smell of pipe tobacco—the signs of their father's recent presence. Max peered into the sink and saw ashes and flakes of tobacco gathered around the drain. Their father never emptied his pipe into the trash can for fear of catching it on fire, so he always tapped it out in the sink. Back home, when their mother wasn't scolding him for smoking, she was scolding him for forgetting to wash the ashes down the drain. For a few months, Max and Carter had even staged an intervention, hiding their father's pipe whenever they could, but he always managed to produce a spare one, as if by magic.

Earlier that morning, just after dawn, the sound of the squeaking floorboards had awakened Max, and she'd made it to the bedroom window in time to see their father's gangly frame as he opened the front gate out onto the street. His glasses were perched askew atop his head as usual, and he was walking lopsidedly with his overstuffed briefcase beneath his arm. In the bed next to Max's, Carter hadn't even stirred.

Now with the kitchen all her own, Max helped herself to what was left of the coffee and picked up one of the German-language newspapers off the table. She liked to play a little game as she flipped through the pages, to see how many English words she could find. She'd just spotted *iPhone* and *Hollywood* when the front doorbell buzzed. It was their housekeeper, Mrs. Amsel, waiting on the stoop with a bag of groceries. She was short and squat and had skin so ruddy and wrinkled it looked like leather. And the woman possessed a terrible habit of speaking her mind.

"Mein Gott!" said Mrs. Amsel in her heavily accented English. "This was on purpose?" She poked one finger up at Max's hair.

"It's just hair," said Max, suddenly and stupidly self-conscious. Why was she embarrassed? Didn't people dye their hair pink because they wanted other people to look at them? Wasn't that the whole point?

"Ah, such things you children do these days," said Mrs. Amsel, shaking her head.

"I didn't think it was a big deal," said Max, just like a carefree girl would. *Care. Free.*

"Mm-hmm," said Mrs. Amsel. "Well, at least the color makes your cheeks look rosy and plump. Very nice."

As the tiny housekeeper brushed past Max and into the house, Max surreptitiously felt her cheeks. "Plump" was certainly not what she was going for.

Their father had hired Mrs. Amsel to tidy up the house they were renting and to cook meals. The woman also kept an eye on Max and her brother, more for their father's peace of mind than anything else, Max suspected.

Mrs. Amsel wiped her forehead with a kerchief. She always wore one over her hair and kept a second one for mopping her sweaty brow. "We're in for a hot day today!" Then she set the brown paper bag on the kitchen table and began arranging plates of cold cuts and thick, whitish sausages. Next she took out a baguette and a hunk of yellow cheese.

"Ah, *meine liebe,* could you bring me a nice sharp knife?"

Max went through the various drawers until she found a long knife with a serrated edge sharp enough for sawing through the thick bread crust. She still didn't know her way around this new kitchen.

"Danke," said Mrs. Amsel, and she began to saw off generous slices of bread. Max had never been able to guess Mrs. Amsel's age. She bustled around with the energy of a young woman, but her hair showed white beneath the scarf, and the loose skin at her elbows wiggled as she sawed the baguette.

"I brought you and your brother a traditional German breakfast. Mr. Weber's children won't starve under my care. And that nice man at the corner grocer gives me a good price on bratwurst."

Everyone Mrs. Amsel talked about was a *nice person.* The nice man who delivered the mail, the nice woman who made change at the bank. *This* nice person and *that* nice person. If Mrs. Amsel was to be believed, then this was the nicest town in all of Europe. But then Max remembered the nice lady at the pharmacy who'd sold her the hair dye. . . . Great, now Max was doing it, too.

When Mrs. Amsel was done setting out the spread, it looked more like a lunch buffet than a breakfast. Cold cuts, sausages, bread and cheese. Max had explained to her several times that she was a vegetarian, but the housekeeper either hadn't understood or was choosing to ignore her. "I'll just have coffee to start, thanks," said Max.

But Mrs. Amsel snatched the coffee mug from Max's hands and slid it to the opposite side of the table, far out of Max's reach. "Coffee stunts your growth," said Mrs. Amsel. "You want to end up small like me? There's juice in the icebox."

As Max dragged herself over to the refrigerator, she wondered how much coffee the diminutive woman had to have drunk to stay that size. She didn't feel like searching the kitchen for a glass, so Max took a long drink of chilled orange juice straight from the bottle. Mrs. Amsel arched her eyebrow at this lack of manners, but she didn't comment on it.

"Did you call your mother last night?"

"We talked online."

"You should call your mother."

Max wanted to tell Mrs. Amsel, for the sixteenth time, that talking to her mother online was better than calling because they could actually see each other, but Mrs. Amsel was willfully ignorant about computers and, it seemed, the twenty-first century in general. No matter what Max said, in Mrs. Amsel's mind, a phone call would always be more personal. Calling your parents when you were away was just the right thing to do.

"Did you tell her about your hair?" asked Mrs. Amsel.

"No," said Max. "I only did it this morning. It was an impulse."

"Mm-hmm," said Mrs. Amsel as she slid a plate piled high with sausages and lunch meat in front of Max's nose.

"And your father?" asked Mrs. Amsel. "What did he say?"

Max tried not to stare at the meat mountain in front of her as she nibbled on a piece of plain bread. She had yet to find a toaster in this house. "Dad came home late and left early. We didn't talk."

Mrs. Amsel didn't answer at first, but poured herself a cup of coffee instead. "Well," she said after she'd spooned enough sugar into her coffee to turn it into syrup. "Mr. Weber is an important man. And very busy. That's why I'm here, *meine liebe*."

"If he's so busy, why'd he drag us halfway across the world with him?" said Max. "I would've been happier with my mom back in New York, not stuck in this stupid place."

Max immediately regretted not that she'd said it, but *how* she'd said it. This *stupid place* was Mrs. Amsel's home, after all. Max took another bite of bread, not wanting to look the housekeeper in the eye. Max's father was ruining her life with this stupid trip of his, but that wasn't Mrs. Amsel's fault.

But if the little woman had taken offense, she didn't show it. "Where is your brother?" she asked as she pushed herself up from the table. "I promised your father I would show you Old Town today, if the walking is not too much for Carter. The boy's breakfast is getting cold."

Max didn't bother pointing out that the traditional German breakfast was mostly cold to begin with.

Mrs. Amsel set off in search of Carter, and the floorboards complained as the little housekeeper hauled herself up the rickety steps. Then Max heard her knock on the bathroom door and her brother's voice loudly respond, "But I just got in here!"

With a quick glance toward the stairs, Max reached for her coffee and stole a sip. It was room temperature, and Max didn't normally take it black, but she didn't feel like searching for the milk, and she was pretty sure Mrs. Amsel had used up all the sugar.

Outside the kitchen window, people were walking briskly along the street, laden with their briefcases and bags as they headed to work, just like back in New York. Cars sped by, and life went on as normally. As Mrs. Amsel had warned, it was turning out to be a hot day already, and Max was wondering if she could figure out how to work the old house's air conditioner when she spotted something across the street. There was movement in the shade of the grocer's awning, and at first she thought it must be a cat, but when it moved out into the sunlight, she recognized it for what it really was—a rat. More than one rat, actually, and they were scurrying about the grocer's fruit stands. What's more, there was a man standing there as well, and though his torso and head were hidden in the shade, Max could tell that he was very tall, and she could clearly see his muddy shoes and the bottom of his long, threadbare coat. Perhaps he was a street person. There were plenty of those back in New York City, but Max had yet to see one here in this tidy little town.

Maybe he was the grocer, and he was content to just let rats play in his food. Max made a mental note to tell Mrs. Amsel not to shop there anymore.

Max was leaning out of the open window to get a better look at the man when her view was suddenly obscured by a group of teenage boys strolling past—laughing and shoving each other as they shared some joke. One of them glanced up at Max, but before they could make eye contact, Max quickly retreated from the window. By the time she looked again, the boys had moved on, and the odd man in the black coat, and the rats, were gone as well.

Max tugged at a pink lock of hair that had fallen in front of her face and examined it between her fingers. It was a soft pink, like baby pajamas. Nothing wild about it at all, really. Just baby-pajamas hair.

"Hamelin stinks," she muttered.

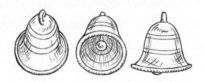

CHAPTER TWO

The worst thing about Carter's sister was that she hadn't always been such a giant pain in the rear end. There was a time, not so long ago, when they'd been friends, not just brother and sister. Back then, coming to this new house their father had rented would have been an adventure. The two of them would have played explorers, searching for hidden rooms and passages. A house this old just had to have secrets.

Now, however, Max spent most of her time alone, and when she was with the family, she was constantly staring at her phone or glaring at nothing at all. Carter had been left to explore on his own, and the house had thus far proved to be depressingly ordinary, though Carter held out hope for the cellar. Still, he would have had a better chance at finding something really interesting if Max had helped. They should have been playing detective and staying up well past his bedtime to tell ghost stories by flashlight. But Carter feared it was too late now for his sister, because the Crouch had gotten hold of her.

Their father taught folklore back in New York City, and what's more, he'd even written books on the subject. That meant Carter and his sister had grown up in a family full of stories. The stories weren't theirs exactly, because their father had collected them from all over the world, but they felt like they belonged to Carter. He had nearly memorized the Grimm brothers' tales by the time he was seven. He'd moved on to the folk stories of Anansi the spider after that, and to Coyote of the Native Americans after that. When Carter finally had exhausted other people's stories, he'd begun making up his own.

Thus was born Carter's legend of the Crouch. An invisible creature, the Crouch preyed upon boys and girls of a certain age—Carter decided seventh graders were a good fit—and would clamber up on top of its victim's shoulders and perch there unseen. It was undetectable to the rest of the world, but the poor adolescent could feel its weight pressing down on her shoulders, forcing her to walk around in a constant slump. The taller the victim grew, the heavier the Crouch became, until it was too much effort to even stand up straight. The Crouch made it so hard to look at the world around you that it was easier to stay slumped over all the time and stare at the floor, or your phone.

But the very worst thing about the Crouch was that it loved to pour malicious lies into its victim's ears. Life was too embarrassing to have any fun, the Crouch whispered. Mothers were embarrassing. Fathers were embarrassing. Little brothers were really embarrassing.

This whole trip to Germany had revealed that Carter's sister was deep in the clutches of a particularly nasty Crouch. This morning's pink hair had probably been the Crouch's idea, too.

Today, led by Mrs. Amsel, Carter and Max were on a tour of Old Town, a walled-off section of Hamelin that had been mostly preserved since medieval times. Here the streets were lined with cobblestones, and the shops looked like ones from a storybook village. Mrs. Amsel told them that some of the sandstone houses dated back four hundred years or more. It was amazing to think that those delicate-looking cottages were older than the United States itself. The town as a whole had been around much longer than that, but most of the buildings had been rebuilt at one time or another over the years. Carter found it impossible to walk down those streets and not feel like he was walking back through time. He liked to pretend he'd been transported to the past, where he was the captain of the town guard, patrolling the streets for brigands and spies.

He'd tried to get Max to play along, but she just rolled her eyes at him and said she didn't even know what a *brigand* was. He would have been happy to tell her that a brigand was just another word for a bandit, but she was too busy listening to the Crouch to listen to Carter.

It was also hard to be the captain of the guard when Mrs. Amsel wouldn't stop fussing over him. Carter couldn't walk twenty feet without the little woman stopping to ask if he needed a rest. It got to be so irritating that when Carter had felt like pausing, when the plastic and metal brace that extended from his left foot to just below his knee had started to rub painfully against his shin, he said nothing. It would have been a simple thing to fix, just tighten the straps, but by the time it'd started to become a real problem, he'd told Mrs. Amsel that he was fine so many times that he didn't want to give her the satisfaction of his admitting he needed to stop.

He knew it was silly, but Carter would happily endure a rub burn rather than prove the woman right.

It wasn't her fault, really, and Mrs. Amsel was kind in her own way. She certainly stuffed the two of them with enough homemade cakes and local sweets to last them for months. But after nine years of walking with a brace, plus one failed surgery, Carter knew best when he needed extra help and when he did not. It was too bad that Mrs. Amsel, like most of the world, didn't always believe him.

Whenever Mrs. Amsel asked Carter if he wanted to rest, Max rolled her eyes at the little housekeeper behind the woman's back, but pointedly enough so that Carter could see. It was a small thing, but it meant a lot to him. It meant that the Crouch hadn't won yet.

The Old Town square turned out to be an open-air plaza filled with café tables and fountains topped with statues. Mrs. Amsel was leading them along a special path of bricks among the cobblestones, each one inlaid with the image of a rat. They served as markers for tourists looking for Hamelin's main attraction—the Pied Piper. Several of the fountains were carved in his likeness, and at least one shop had

Pied Piper Monopoly sets for sale in the window. Carter would have to convince his father to buy him one of those before they went home to New York.

The stone rats led them to an ancient house on a corner, with an arched wooden doorway framed by two gaslight lanterns. The building was topped with a pointed slate roof, but something in the angles of it looked all wrong to Carter, as if the lines zigzagged unnecessarily. It wasn't the kind of thing he liked staring at, and from the various nooks and crannies, puckered stone faces leered at passersby. But there was a welcome bench outside the house, and Carter finally took the opportunity to rest his leg and adjust the straps on his brace.

"This is the Rattenfängerhaus," said Mrs. Amsel.

"What's a Ratten-whatever?" Max asked.

"The ratcatcher's house," said Mrs. Amsel. "The house named for the Pied Piper. This one is very interesting for your father, I think."

"Then I don't really care," said Max.

Carter wished his sister wouldn't talk like that. Their father was working on an important book about the town legend, and while it was true that this was the first research trip their mother hadn't accompanied them on, Max was taking their mother's absence personally, as if their father had done something wrong. Carter wasn't happy that their father was too busy to spend time with them, but he wasn't punishing other people for it. Max had gotten it into her stubborn head that she needed to be uninterested in everything her father might be interested in, including the Pied Piper. Which was going to be hard because, as far as Carter could tell, Hamelin was one big Pied Piper tourist trap.

"There are a lot of gargoyles on that house," said Carter, craning his neck to get a good look at the grimacing statues.

"To scare away the spirits of the dark forest," said Mrs. Amsel. "The forest held many dangers. From mischievous kobolds that would butter your shoes when you were sleeping to wood witches who liked nothing better than to bake children into pies! People back then were afraid of the dark magic of the world, not just wolves and brigands."

At the mention of the word *brigands,* Carter gave his sister a smug nod. "That means bandits," he whispered. Max ignored him.

"Back home there are faces in the architecture everywhere, all over New York City," Carter told Mrs. Amsel. "Faces covered in leaves, called green men. Dad points them out to us all the time."

"And do people believe in these green men still?" asked Mrs. Amsel.

"No," said Carter. "Most people don't even realize they're there."

"People can look at so much and yet they see nothing," laughed Mrs. Amsel. "It is the same with us. Too few remember the past. Especially the young."

"Oh, come on," said Max. "And what—this is supposed to be the Pied Piper's real house?"

"Oh, no," said Mrs. Amsel. "This house was built in the sixteen hundreds, long after the piper's time."

"Yeah, and the Pied Piper is just a fairy tale!" said Max. "Where's Little Red Riding Hood's penthouse? Around here somewhere?"

Mrs. Amsel placed her hands on her hips. *"Am vielen Lachen erkennt man den Narren,"* she said, shaking her head. "You want to know why we call it the Piper's House, *mein lieber*? Come, I will show you."

Carter hauled himself back to his feet before Mrs. Amsel could ask if he was ready to walk, but his leg was much better now that he'd fitted the strap correctly. The housekeeper led the two of them away from the front of the house to a narrow side street. Unlike the rest of the town square, where there were raucous crowds and street performers everywhere, this little avenue was quiet and mostly empty except for a few tourists taking pictures. They were gathered around a plaque set into the side of the Piper's House. One of them, a man with a bulky camera and hip pouch, was trying to be discreet as he stared at Carter's leg. It was left to Carter to pretend not to notice.

"This street is called Bungelosenstrasse," said Mrs. Amsel, softly. "No one dances here, or plays music. We keep our voices low, out of respect."

"Why?" asked Max.

"Because this street is where he took them," said Mrs. Amsel. "Look there."

Mrs. Amsel pointed to the plaque, which was written in German. "In English, roughly, it says:

> *In the year 1284 after the birth of Christ*
> *From Hamelin were led away*
> *One hundred thirty children, born at this place*
> *Led away by a piper into a mountain."*

Carter was glad when she reached the end. Of course, he loved stories, but something about hearing those words spoken aloud, especially on this strangely quiet street, gave him goose bumps.

It had less of an effect on his sister. "Why's this town so crazy about one fairy tale?" Max asked. "This is just for the tourists, right?"

"Ah," said Mrs. Amsel. "But this is not a fairy tale."

"You're not telling me you believe it?" asked Max. "That a magic piper stole all Hamelin's children away?"

Mrs. Amsel squinted at her. "That doesn't make it a fairy tale," she said. "Fairy tales have happy endings."

"Mrs. Amsel," said Carter. "You know a lot about this stuff."

"All Hameliners know the story of the Pied Piper," she said.

"Yeah, but you know a lot. Are you a folklorist like our dad?"

"Hmph," said Mrs. Amsel. "Your father is an important man. I am just a housekeeper. Now come, we don't want to be late."

Mrs. Amsel turned and led them away from Bungelosen-strasse, and as they walked, Carter caught his sister's eye and mouthed, *What's the matter with you?*

Max mouthed back, *She's senile,* and made a crazy gesture with her finger.

Hopeless.

They followed their housekeeper until they reached a small stage that had been erected in the center of the plaza. Paper lanterns were strung from the trees, and behind the stage, a giant curtain painted to look like a mountain range hung as a backdrop. Crowds of tourists, and even a few locals, were gathered in front of it, waiting patiently. Street vendors passed in and out of the crowd, selling sweets and souvenirs.

"What are we waiting for?" asked Max. "*Rats* the musical?"

"Today is June twenty-sixth," said Mrs. Amsel.

"Oh!" said Carter. "That's the anniversary of the story! Dad told me."

Mrs. Amsel nodded. "We put on a play every year for the tourists, but the children enjoy it, too."

While they waited for the show to begin, Mrs. Amsel waved over a vendor and bought each of them a pack of black licorice rats. Max made a face as Carter managed to fit three into his mouth at once. He let the tails dangle over his chin.

"Ugh, disgusting," she said. "Here, you can have mine."

"Mission accomplished," mumbled Carter past a mouthful of gummy rats.

As church bells began to ring, the crowd quieted and the rat vendors ceased their calls. Everyone's attention turned to the little stage as an elderly couple dressed in colorful frocks and garish stage makeup entered through the curtain. The round little man put his arms around his plump wife.

"He is not the sort of person who should be wearing tights," whispered Max.

The man was talking to the audience, delivering his lines in German.

"Lean close, children," Mrs. Amsel said softly. "I will translate the story for you."

Carter did as he was told, but his sister stayed where she was, arms crossed defiantly across her chest.

"Once upon a time," said Mrs. Amsel. "The village of Hamelin was overrun with rats." Right then the curtains parted, and the rats—who were actually just children dressed in felt rat costumes—scurried onstage.

"Oh, would you look at them?" cried Mrs. Amsel. "Such dears!" The children were trying their best to look menacing, but they couldn't see very well in their floppy rat masks—the snouts dangled in front of their eyes—and they kept bumping into each other. The audience was breaking out in giggles.

"Oh, but here comes the important part," said Mrs. Amsel, suddenly serious when a man dressed in a clownish red, yellow and green cloak took the stage. "One night," continued Mrs. Amsel, "it seemed the villagers' prayers for deliverance were answered, and a piper in a pied coat arrived and offered to rid the village of the rats once and for all. The town elders were desperate, even though the Piper had asked for a fee that not even a king could pay. Nevertheless, they agreed to his terms, and they watched, amazed, as the Piper began to play and the rats answered his call. Throughout the village he danced, and the rats followed. He led them to the river Weser, and there they drowned."

As Mrs. Amsel narrated, the Piper onstage played and the rats danced around him until one by one they disappeared behind a new backdrop curtain that had been painted to look like a river winding through the countryside.

"The Piper returned to the elders and demanded his payment, but the villagers could not afford such a sum. They offered to pay him what they could spare, but it was only a fraction of what he'd demanded. The Piper swore vengeance.

"Now the village elders, in their pride, were not afraid of the Piper. The rats were dead, drowned in the river, so what could one angry Piper do to them? They laughed at his threats and decided to pay him nothing at all.

"They were fools." Mrs. Amsel pointed to the Piper on-stage and whispered, "Watch."

The Piper began to play again, only this time the song was slower, more melancholy than before. The curtain rose once more, revealing the children, changed out of their rat costumes and sleeping soundly in their beds. Carter expected the audience to respond, to *ooh* and *aah* at the adorable sleeping children, but no one said a word. They were rapt, their attention on the play. Carter's was on Mrs. Amsel. She was whispering so softly now that he had to lean in very close to hear. He was surprised to find his sister leaning in, too.

"The Piper stole back to Hamelin in the late hours of night," whispered Mrs. Amsel. "And he played a new song. This time, as he danced throughout the village, it was the children who answered his call. Across the square and along the Bungelosenstrasse, they danced, through the gate and beyond, into the mountains, where they disappeared."

As Mrs. Amsel narrated, the Piper actor and the children did actually dance off the stage and through the square until they reached the Bungelosenstrasse, the quiet street. Then he stopped playing, and they marched solemnly away.

"All the children who could walk followed him, all but one," said Mrs. Amsel, and at this Carter noticed that one boy had been left behind—a small boy who walked with crutches. He'd tried to keep up, but the procession was too fast for him and he was left in the square alone.

Carter could feel Mrs. Amsel's eyes on him as he watched the boy struggle to catch up. She sounded hesitant to continue. "The boy who was left behind ... he told the villagers what had occurred, and it is thanks to him that Hamelin knows what became of its children, even if they are lost forever."

Mrs. Amsel cleared her throat. "Or so the story goes."

Carter felt his cheeks burning as he shifted uneasily. He winced as his brace banged against a wrought iron streetlamp. At the sound, several heads turned his way.

His sister was next to him. He could feel her watching him. "What?" he said. "I'm fine."

That was a lie. He knew the story of the Pied Piper well enough to know that there was always a boy who got left behind, someone who could tell the tale. But in the versions he'd read, it had been a blind boy who'd gotten lost trying to follow the others, or a deaf boy who couldn't hear the music at all. This version was new to him. This *boy* was new to him. When the boy had first appeared onstage, Carter had thought, or he'd hoped, that the boy might turn out to be a hero and break the Piper's spell or something like that. But that wasn't how the story ended. It ended with the boy left behind. Carter felt stupid himself for wishing anything different.

"I'm fine," he told his sister again.

"Okay," Max said, sounding uncertain.

"Really, I said I'm fine!"

"And I said okay!"

Then the song was over. The stage curtain drew closed and the audience around them started to applaud. Max was still watching Carter, and it wasn't until he started clapping that she joined in, too.

CHAPTER THREE

M ax's mind had wandered throughout much of the first half of the play as she wondered what her friends were doing back home and whether their mother was lonely in their empty apartment. But the play's ending had taken a disturbing turn, one that had been hard to ignore. That was the thing she hated about the stories her dad collected—they might seem charming and magical, but there was usually something dark hiding just beneath the surface. Sure Hansel and Gretel defeated the witch in the end, but they'd gotten lost in the forest in the first place because their parents had abandoned them there. Little Red was saved by the huntsman but not until after the wolf had devoured her grandmother. And the townsfolk of Hamelin refused to pay the Piper, so their children had to pay the price.

As the audience dispersed, Max glanced over at the street vendors hawking their wares. It was a horrible thing to be selling souvenirs of such a terrible story. Then there was that part at the end with the boy who was left behind. Max watched Carter closely after that. Her little brother was tough, tougher than most people gave him credit for, but sometimes when you weren't expecting something was when it hit you the hardest, and neither of them had been expecting that. Max had spent many years sticking up for her younger brother. She'd faced down more than one ignorant jerk who had decided to target Carter because he was different. As he got older, Carter had learned how to stick up for himself. "Words only hurt if you let them," he'd say. But sometimes things people say are sharp enough to cut no matter how thick you think your skin is.

Her brother was a tough kid, but he was still only a kid.

Carter insisted he was fine, however, so Max decided to let it go. He already had one little old lady hovering over him; he didn't need another.

The Piper and the children had returned to the stage to take their bows, and now they were mingling with the crowd. The actor who'd played the Piper played his flute for the tourists' kids and posed for pictures. Who wouldn't want a picture of their child with the child catcher?

"Where's the kid on the crutches?" asked Carter.

"I dunno," said Max, looking around. "He must be here somewhere."

"I'm going to look for him," said Carter.

"Don't wander off," said Mrs. Amsel. She was red-faced and sweaty and sat down heavily on a bench. "This heat! I'll rest a minute, but you children stay together and don't leave the plaza."

Max followed her brother as he searched for the boy, but they hadn't gotten far when they were waylaid by a street performer juggling fire sticks over his head.

"*Guten tag, mein liebe,*" said the young man as Max walked around him, trying to give him and his fire sticks a wide berth.

"I'm sorry, I don't speak German," Max said.

"Ah, American?" said the juggler, smiling. He was dressed in a jester's motley outfit, the tassels topped with little bells like fairy chimes. "Do you like magic?"

Max thought about the magic in her father's stories, and in the play they'd just seen. Magic rarely led to good in those tales, but of course that wasn't the kind of magic this young man was referring to.

"Do you know any card tricks?" Max asked. The juggler laughed, even as he twirled a fire stick over his head and caught it again. Several nearby people clapped for him.

"Magic is magic, if you believe in it," he said. "Watch!" Then the fire began to change color. As he spun the torches expertly into the air, the flames changed from orange to blue, to green and, lastly, to purple.

There was more excited applause, and Max supposed it was only polite to join in. It was certainly a nice trick. The juggler must've treated his fire sticks with some kind of chemical that changed color when it burned, though Max had to admit that she couldn't remember ever seeing a purple flame before.

She'd just turned around to ask her brother if he had any theories about the color-changing fire (Carter was full of theories about everything) when she realized he was gone. He was so much shorter than the rest of the adults, it was hard to know if he'd wandered just a few feet away or to the other side of the plaza. "Carter?"

"Look! Look!" said the juggler. "I have more magic, my American girl!"

Max ignored the street performer as she pushed through the crowd, searching for her brother. Mrs. Amsel had specifically told them to stay together, and Max didn't feel like getting a lecture from their housekeeper today. The longer Max went without finding him, the more annoyed she got.

"Carter! Carter!"

Finally she spotted him. He'd wandered over to the Piper's House. Why had he left in the first place? Was he trying to get her in trouble? Then, as Max started to make her way over to him, she spotted something troubling. Across from the Piper's House, an alley opened onto the quiet street, and at this time of day, with the sun sinking low, that alley was little more than a pool of shadow. Something in the alley moved. It was just a shuffle of feet stepping into the sunlight and the swaying of a ragged coat in the breeze. A figure in a long black coat was standing there, mostly hidden in the shadows, just feet from her brother.

Max stepped up her pace to a run. Carter was walking toward the Bungelosenstrasse, and toward that alley. He was probably still looking for the boy, and he wasn't watching where he was going. The man in the alley took a step forward but seemed reluctant to leave the shade.

"Carter!" Max shouted. It was enough that heads turned her way and one of the street musicians stopped strumming his guitar as he looked around to see what the commotion was about.

"What?" said her brother, looking at her.

The man retreated a few steps into the alley. Max caught up to her brother and grabbed him by the wrist, more roughly than she'd meant to.

"Ow!" he cried. "What's your problem?"

"Why'd you wander off like that?" said Max. Her heart was beating fast in her chest and she felt a little sick. "I couldn't find you anywhere!"

"Mrs. Amsel said to stay in the plaza," he protested. "I'm in the plaza."

Max looked over her brother's shoulder. The man was still there, only some twenty feet away, but hard to get a good look at because of the way he hugged the shadows. Although there were no rats this time, Max was sure it was the same man she'd seen this morning at the fruit stand across from their house. She recognized the black coat and the filthy shoes.

"What are you looking at?" asked Carter, following her gaze.

"I've seen that man before," Max whispered. "He was outside our house this morning."

"Are you sure?" said Carter. "I can't get a good look at him."

"I'm sure. Come on, I want to get out of here."

Thankfully, Carter didn't argue with her, and the two of them set off to find Mrs. Amsel. As they walked, Max glanced back over her shoulder several times to see if the man in the black coat had moved from his place in the shadows, to see if he'd dared to come out into the sun. He hadn't.

⟨CHAPTER FOUR⟩

"Hamelin is not like New York City," Mrs. Amsel was saying. "But we sometimes get drifters looking to beg money off the tourists. Vagrants. Most are harmless, poor souls, but you children are right to stay away."

Carter knew that his sister hadn't wanted to tell Mrs. Amsel about the man in the alley, but if the man had scared his sister that much, Carter figured Mrs. Amsel should know about it. The housekeeper said she was more concerned that the children had gotten separated, and vowed to keep them on a shorter leash next time. But even as she told them not to worry overly much about the strange man, she continued to interrogate them about every last detail. She made them repeat over and over again what they'd seen, almost as if she were looking for holes in their story, but there really wasn't much else to tell. Like Max, Carter had been able to make out only the shoes and part of a torn black coat.

Carter could tell that Max was still sore at him for wandering away in the first place, and more for telling Mrs. Amsel about it afterward. Whenever he tried to make conversation, she glowered at him, but he honestly hadn't meant to wander that far. It was just easy to get lost in all the crowds.

He did finally locate the boy from the play. As they were walking home, Carter spotted him sharing a pizza with his parents at an outdoor café. Out of costume, the boy looked to be about Carter's age, or maybe a year or two younger, even. As they got closer, the boy must've noticed Carter staring at him, because he waved. He seemed friendly enough, so Carter, Mrs. Amsel and Max stopped at their table.

"You were really good in the play," said Carter. The boy didn't speak English, so Mrs. Amsel translated.

At once, the boy's face lit up with pleasure, and his mother reached over and planted a proud kiss on his cheek. *"Danke,"* said the boy.

"Bitte," answered Carter. He'd picked up enough German to say *you're welcome,* at least. Then the boy stood up and reached out to shake Carter's hand. That's when Carter saw that the boy didn't have any crutches and that he had no problem stepping over his chair to get to Carter. *Of course.* The boy was an actor, and the crutches had been part of the act, too. Carter surprised himself at how disappointed and, in some way, just a little betrayed he felt.

Then there was an uncomfortable moment when the boy noticed Carter's limp for the first time and, worse, Carter saw him notice it.

Since they were already outside the café, Mrs. Amsel

went inside to buy them a pizza for dinner. Carter suggested they get it to go; he no longer felt like staying around and chatting. As they left, Carter called goodbye to the boy and his parents. He could say that in German, too.

Mrs. Amsel complained that there was a criminal lack of plates and flatware back at the rental house, so she picked up paper plates and cups on the way home. Back in the kitchen, she served up the pizza on disposable plates decorated with winged horses in party hats. As she passed a slice to his sister, Carter had to smile because he couldn't think of anything more un-Max-like than those cute horses with wings.

"Great plates," said Max. "I would've loved these when I was five."

"They were on sale," Mrs. Amsel said. "It was winged horses or robots."

"Robots are cool," mumbled Carter as he shoved a slice into his mouth. Why bother waiting for a plate?

"I'm surprised you could find anything that wasn't decorated with rats in this town," said Max. "Anyway, they're Pegasuses."

Carter stopped chewing and looked at her. "Wha—?"

"That's what the flying horses are called," Max said, shrugging. "Greek myth. The favored horses of Zeus. Or maybe the plural is *Pegasi,* I'm not sure."

Carter continued to stare.

"What?" she said. "He's my dad, too. I'm bound to pick up some useless nerd trivia from this family, whether I like it or not."

"I think it's very interesting," said Mrs. Amsel, and Carter went back to chewing. He couldn't be sure, but he'd thought that maybe, for just a second, Max had managed to get the Crouch to lighten up a bit.

After that, everybody relaxed a little, the play and the shadow man finally forgotten. Before long, there was nothing left on the table but a few pizza crusts. Mrs. Amsel produced one of her homemade cakes for dessert, and not even Max could think of anything to complain about that. As Mrs. Amsel cut into the cake, she swore in German as a bead of sweat dripped off her chin dangerously close to the cake. "Oh, pardon me," she said. "I am melting in this weather."

"I think there's an air conditioner," said Max. "The thermostat's on the wall over there, but I haven't tried it out."

"I wouldn't want to turn it on without your father's permission," said Mrs. Amsel.

"It's not like he's going to care, or even notice," said Max.

"I'll do it!" said Carter, jumping up. He liked to push buttons.

Carter picked up his piece of cake with his fingers and shoved a full half of it into his mouth as he left the table. As he passed his sister, he opened his mouth to show her his "see food."

"Neanderthal," Max whispered at him, and Carter snorted a small cloud of cake crumbs at her. He examined the thermostat for a minute and then punched a few unmarked buttons, ones he hoped were Cool and On.

"Let me get the window," said Max, and she shut and locked the kitchen window as a muffled metallic clunk came from somewhere under the floor, followed by the hum of cool air wafting through the vents.

And then something else. A faint sound, but one that

definitely didn't belong. Like the pitter-patter of raindrops on a tin roof. "What'd you do?" said Max. "Break it?"

But the noise was already changing, getting louder. "Ah!" said Mrs. Amsel. "What is that sound?"

Carter listened at the vent. The noise was coming from somewhere below, growing louder and louder until the raindrops sounded like a hailstorm inside the walls. Carter put his face up to the vent and peered inside.

What he saw caused him to cry out and tumble backward on his bad leg, barely dodging the air vent when it came bursting off the wall as hundreds, if not thousands, of beady eyes, filthy whiskers and wormlike tails spilled from that dark tunnel. Rats, pouring into the kitchen. So, so many rats.

Everyone started screaming as the floor disappeared beneath the wave of rodents. Mrs. Amsel shrieked louder than anyone else as she hauled herself up onto her chair. Max and Carter tried to kick away the mass of wriggling rodents at their feet, but when they kicked one, three more took its place.

One part of Carter's brain—unfortunately, the part mostly in control—was as hysterical as everyone else's. The rats, with their sleek bodies and grotesquely human-like hands, inspired some kind of instinctive revulsion, a blind fear. But somewhere else in the back of his head a memory shook loose, a fact he'd read somewhere that had stuck.

What is a horde of rats called? he asked himself. *Oh yes, it's called a mischief. What a perfect name for what they are. A mischief of rats.*

Max was calling Carter's name, snapping him back to the here and now. "Help me get the door!" she was shouting.

The rats were massing up against the front door. Piling over each other as they launched themselves at the wooden frame, scratching and biting at the cracks. Max had managed to put the coat stand between her and the growing tangle of scurrying bodies.

And what was Carter supposed to do about all this?

Then he saw what she was pointing at—the doorknob was just high enough to be beyond the reach of biting teeth. With a yell, Carter grabbed for the handle. Max stepped out of her hiding place to kick a path clear for him with the heavy black boots she wore everywhere. Carter grabbed the knob and swung the door open wide.

Like water escaping from a punctured tank, the rats poured out of the house. En masse, they streamed into the fading day, crossed the street and disappeared into the sewer grates. It was an almost orderly retreat, if not quite done in single file, and within minutes they had all vanished. The street itself was strangely quiet, empty of traffic. The only evidence of the rats having been there at all was the ruined vent in the kitchen and thousands of dirty rat paw prints crisscrossing the floor.

No one spoke at first, and the only sound to be heard was their own heavy breathing. Carter couldn't take his eyes off the street. Not a soul was in sight, and there wasn't a hint of a breeze to disturb the near-perfect stillness. Where had everyone gone?

As if in answer to his unspoken question, a car turned the corner. Then another. Voices echoed from nearby as one of the neighbors laughed at her evening television program. Someone else's radio was up too loud. It was as if the town had paused to hold its breath and was only now letting it out. As his sister joined him at the doorway, Carter watched her look to the sewer grates where the rats had fled, then over at the storefront where she'd seen the man earlier. He knew what she was thinking, but it was empty now.

Carter and his sister exchanged a long look; then they turned back to Mrs. Amsel. Their housekeeper was white and shaking, but unhurt.

"*Mein Gott,*" she said. "Are you children all right?"

They both nodded, standing there dumbly. Finally, Carter leaned over and whispered to his sister, "So rats, huh?"

❧ CHAPTER FIVE ❧

Sleep was far, far away. How could Max sleep when the day kept playing over and over again in her brain in a loop? Every time she closed her eyes, she saw the rats swarming around her, and her heart beat so loudly in her ears that she wrapped a pillow around her head to try and drown it out. How had she not heard it before? How did she manage to make it through every day without going deaf from the ceaseless racket of her own heartbeat?

Crazy, late-night thoughts.

Carter, on the other hand, had proven once again that he could fall asleep at any time and under any circumstances. After long car rides, their mother and father still had to carry him up to bed, unconscious, like a baby. You could strip him down and change him into his pajamas and he wouldn't so much as twitch.

Mrs. Amsel insisted on staying until their father came

home, although when that would be was anyone's guess. He'd had his phone turned off all evening, and even though their housekeeper had left him at least five frantic messages in a mix of panicked English and German, they still hadn't heard from him by the time she shooed the children up to bed. By the third time Max had gotten up for a glass of water, Mrs. Amsel had fallen asleep in a chair by the living room window, her chin resting on her chest. Max climbed back into her bed and stared at the ceiling. It is one of the loneliest feelings in the world, to be the only one awake in a house full of sleeping people.

After a couple of hours, Max decided that lying in her bed wide-awake was pointless. She'd go down and wake Mrs. Amsel, and tell the old housekeeper to go home and get some real rest. Max might as well wait up for her father, since she wasn't sleeping anyway, and poor Mrs. Amsel had already been through enough for one day.

Max tiptoed out of the bedroom, mindful of the squeaking boards in the hallway, and made her way down the stairs. She didn't know why she felt the need to be quiet, since her brother wouldn't waken for anything less than a siren going off next to his face. But an old house at night feels like it deserves silence, somehow.

On this quiet night, the moon cast pools of blue light through the downstairs windows, but the floors were mostly hidden in inky blackness. Just dark enough to hide a rat or two.

Max was very aware of her exposed little toes as she pattered across the lightless hallway, toward the living room. She wished she had her boots on, but who thinks to put on boots just to go downstairs?

She fumbled for the light switch on the living room wall but only succeeded in toppling over a small vase of flowers on one of the end tables. This was silly. Her imagination had worked itself into such a panic that she couldn't even find a simple light switch. That's when she noticed the figure framed by the moonlight. It was a tall shape, sitting upright and alert in the chair against the window. It was facing her, and it was definitely not Mrs. Amsel.

Max might have cried out, except that she caught a whiff of something, the smoke of her father's tobacco pipe. The bowl glowed orange in the dark as he inhaled. "It's all right, Max," he said. "It's only me."

Her father turned on a small table lamp, and Max had to squint as her vision briefly danced with purple bulb-shaped spots. "I didn't hear you come home," she said.

"I tried to be quiet," said her father. "I didn't want to wake you and your brother." Her father smiled at her, glasses perched on his forehead and his pipe sticking out between the tobacco-stained whiskers of his mustache and beard. Max knew that the same kids back in New York who teased Carter about his leg also made fun of him because their father was older than the other kids' dads—they called him *grandpa*. Max's sore point wasn't their father's age but his slovenly appearance. He would often get so caught up in his work that he would forget to change into clean clothes or comb his hair. Maybe it wasn't his fault, or maybe he just couldn't be bothered to remember. Whatever the case, tonight he looked more rumpled than usual. There were dark bags under his eyes that shouldn't have been there, and Max didn't want to know how many days in a row he'd been wearing that same sweat-stained shirt.

This wouldn't have been a problem if their mother had been around. She was always the one making him close his books at night and reminding him to go to bed at a reasonable hour. Carter took after their father in that way— always thinking, always off dreaming somewhere among the clouds. It was Mom who kept everyone tethered to the ground.

"I couldn't sleep anyway," said Max, and she gestured in the direction of the kitchen.

"Yes, Mrs. Amsel filled me in on everything," said her father. "I'm so sorry, Max. I had my phone off because I was working in the special collection over at the hall of records. Did you know that some of the documents there are so old you have to wear surgical gloves? . . . Anyway, I'm sorry."

Max shrugged. "Mrs. Amsel taped some tinfoil over the vent. I don't think that's going to cut it, though."

"I told her to go home and get some sleep," said her father, nodding. "I had to practically push her out the door. And I told her to take tomorrow off, no discussion." Their father was going to make Carter and her stay home alone? With the rats and everything?

He read the look of alarm on his daughter's face. "I'm staying here, too," he said. "I called the landlord to tell him about what happened, and he's sending over an exterminator in the morning. Hopefully one who speaks English."

Her father sounded perfectly calm, even reassuring, as he talked, but Max noticed that he kept sneaking little glances out the window, as if he were watching for something out there. Or someone.

"Dad, why were you sitting here in the dark?"

"I was just thinking," he said, tapping the bowl of his pipe. The tobacco had gone out. "It's too hot upstairs and, well, I don't feel like trying out the AC again."

Max nodded. The upstairs was sweltering, but that didn't explain why he had the lights off, and the way he kept checking over his shoulder made her suspect that he wasn't being one hundred percent honest with her. Max had an idea what he was looking for.

"Dad, did Mrs. Amsel tell you about the man I saw today?"

Max's father stiffened in his chair. "Yes, she did," he said. "She told me that you two disobeyed her instructions to stay together, too. Max, you should know better than to let your brother wander off alone."

Her father was trying to change the subject by playing the part of the scolding parent, but Max wasn't going to let him get away with it. "Dad, were you sitting here in the dark because you were looking out for that man?"

Max's father leaned forward like he might protest but then sank back into his chair, deflated. "I don't know who that was," he said quietly. "And Mrs. Amsel is probably right that it was just a homeless person."

Max went to the window. The streetlights were on but there was hardly anyone around. Not anyone that she could see, at least.

"Sit down, kiddo," her father said, and he pulled up a

footstool. *Kiddo.* He hadn't called her that in some time. Her father lowered the window blinds.

"You know my job's not a dangerous one," he said. "And I would never do anything to put you and your brother at any kind of risk, you know that, right?"

"Um, no offense, Dad," said Max, "but you collect fairy tales. I used to tell kids you were a spy when I was little just so that I wouldn't get picked on at recess."

Her father nodded.

"You're not, are you?" Max asked quickly.

"No," laughed her father. "I'm not a spy. Paper cuts are about as perilous as my job usually gets. But still, in the stuffy world of academia, there's money to be made. Even fame, for those very lucky few who manage to discover something new."

"Like what?"

Her father pushed his glasses farther up on his forehead and leaned closer. "Shakespeare wrote thirty-seven plays in his lifetime that have survived. But we know from records that he wrote more than that. We have the title of at least one, called *Love's Labor's Won,* but no copy survives, at least not one that's been discovered. How much do you think that play would be worth today?"

"A lot?"

"Priceless. And the person who found it . . . well, they'd be a rock star. In the bookish sense, of course."

Max frowned, considering this. "But you teach folklore. Have you found some lost fairy tale or something?"

"Maybe, at least I think so," said her father, his voice

quickening. "It's why I came all the way here to Hamelin. As I was researching my book on the Pied Piper legend, I met a man who showed me something remarkable." Her father stood up and peeked out through the blinds; then he began pacing around the room.

"I've told you before how the Grimm brothers only wrote down the stories that they'd been hearing for years? They took the oral tales of this region in particular, stories of the dark forest and the mountains, and collected them in books. But those stories had been around for hundreds of years before that. Well, take a look at this."

Her father opened his briefcase. It was a sentimental leather case, with a well-worn handle and brass latches that had turned green over the years. Very gently, carefully, her father pulled out a yellowed piece of paper protected by a plastic cover. There was writing down the middle, and a scrollwork of illustrations along the top and bottom, like a page in a book. It looked very old.

"How's your German coming along?"

"I can order a hot dog with sauerkraut," said Max.

"Well, then allow me to translate. What you're looking at is the table of contents from a very early, very limited edition of the Grimm brothers' book *Children's and Household Tales*. We know that there were seven versions of the book published, with the last one in 1857. But if this table of contents is authentic, then there was an eighth version—one that predated all the others, and it's one with a small but significant difference."

Her father pointed to a line on the ancient, yellowed

page. Besides being in German, the ink was so faded and the handwriting so archaic that she couldn't possibly read it.

"This table of contents lists a story that doesn't appear in any other of the surviving editions," explained her father. "A story called 'The Piper and the Peddler.'"

"Doesn't sound too great to me."

"But it is. If this is a lost tale, a folk story that was edited out for some reason, that would be the find of a lifetime."

"I get it," said Max. "That would be a super big deal in your field. So you came here to Hamelin to find this lost fairy tale. And did you? Did you find it?"

"Not yet," said her father quietly, and again he glanced over at the window. "But I might have found something even more incredible."

He took Max's hand and pulled her close, as if whatever he was about to say, he didn't want to say it too loudly. "All these stories," he said. "Generations of stories, and they all started the same way—as lessons. Made-up fables designed to teach us right from wrong, that sort of thing."

"Right, like don't eat a witch's gingerbread house."

"But what if one of those stories wasn't just a fable?" said her father. "What if one of those fairy tales wasn't a fairy tale at all, and what if I could prove it?"

Max pulled back a little from her father. Something in his stare, in those sleep-starved eyes, made her worried for him. And not just because he was sounding more and more like he really thought he was in some kind of spy thriller. He didn't look good, and he didn't look healthy. Again Max wished her mother were here, now more than ever.

"So . . . what did you find?" she asked cautiously.

Her father pulled another document from inside his briefcase. If anything, this one looked older than the page from the Brothers Grimm book. "A page from a young Hameliner's journal," said her father. "Dated 1284—the same year the children of Hamelin were supposedly taken. The story the boy tells is outlandish, of course. He was probably the victim of mental illness, or maybe it was a case of mass hysteria. Or maybe he was just a very creative liar, but it is still the undeniable origin of the story of the Pied Piper. It's as if someone had found the story of Little Red Riding Hood signed by the author!"

"And that's an even bigger deal?"

Her father nodded. "And it's real, Max. I've shared it with a few experts, enough to verify its authenticity." Her father stood up and crossed to the window yet again, peering through the blinds.

"I haven't told many people, but I suppose if the wrong sort of person heard about it . . ." Her father paused. "After Mrs. Amsel told me about what you'd seen today, about the man across the street, and the one in the plaza, it got me thinking."

"Wait," said Max. "You don't think that homeless guy I saw is after your research?"

"No," said her father, sighing. "I don't know. Who knows what people are capable of if they want something badly enough. Paying people to spy on us, even setting a bunch of rats loose in our house to scare us off. All I know is, I don't want you and your brother staying here any longer."

"You're sending us away?"

"Back to New York. I shouldn't have brought you in the first place."

Max wasn't sure how she should respond. Up until this very moment, Max's relationship with her father could have best been described as *distracted*. He was a kind man, witty and generous when the mood took him, but he was rarely present. He might be physically in the same room with you, but part of him was always lost in his books, in someone else's stories. Even as he asked how his children's day had been, even as he kissed Max good night on the forehead, she was never sure if he was thinking about her or if he was thinking about tomorrow's lecture. But right now, he was here—all of him, here. Max was being invited to share in his obsession, and therefore she had all of his attention.

It was just too bad that his story was so unbelievable. What sort of person stalked another person's children because of some old fairy tale? And who would possibly go through the effort of setting up an elaborate hoax like the rats in the walls? Who *could* do such a thing? It all sounded outlandish to Max, and while she was afraid of that shadowy man she'd seen, she had a hard time believing he was part of some conspiracy to steal her father's work. More likely he was just some nutcase, wandering the town and scaring anyone and everyone who crossed his path.

Her father needed sleep and a hot meal. If nothing else came of that awful day, at least he would be taking tomorrow off to stay at home with them. That might be exactly the rest Max's father needed. But tonight, if he was in the rare mood to be honest with her, whether it was from exhaustion or something else, Max decided to take advantage of it. There was something she'd been wanting to ask him but hadn't yet found the time or the courage to do it.

"Dad? Why didn't Mom come with us to Germany?"

Her father paused before answering. "She had things she wanted to get done. We've been over this."

He was avoiding something, turning his attention suddenly to his shoes, his watch, not looking his daughter in the eye, but Max pressed him. "She's always come with us before. All those trips, she never stayed behind. Not once."

Max's father looked at her, and something behind his eyes melted. "You have to understand, Max, that sometimes adults need . . . space to figure things out. Your mom just needed her space, is all."

"Space from you or from us?"

"From me," said her father, and he gently put both hands on her shoulders. "You have to believe that, okay? This has nothing to do with how she feels about you and your brother. I've been very busy, maybe too busy, and she just thought that maybe the three of us alone together would do us all some good."

He gave her shoulders a squeeze. "I've not done a very good job of it so far, have I?"

Max's father had always been lanky, with wiry arms that hung well past his shirt cuffs. But as she felt his bony fingers on her shoulders and stared into the deep hollow of his neck, she realized he'd gotten too skinny, almost gaunt, in the last few weeks. It was hard to see her father look so fragile, and it scared her more than rats or men in the shadows. "Dad?" pleaded Max. "Can we all just go home? All of us, please?"

Her father looked at her, then back to the window. Would he peek one last time at the street, looking for the man who wasn't there? Or would he answer his daughter this very important question, his daughter who hardly ever asked him for anything at all?

He took off his glasses and rubbed his eyes. "I'll call the airline tomorrow," he said at last. "Give me just a few days to tie things up here, but we'll be back in New York by the end of the week."

He looked like he might hug her, like he wanted to, but Max's father had never been good at expressions of affection. The most he managed that night was a pat on her shoulder, but it was something. "By the way," he said. "I do like the new hair."

"I haven't decided if I'm going to keep it."

"You know, your mom had a green stripe in her hair once, back before we were married."

Max looked at her father in disbelief. "Mom?"

Her father nodded, smiling. "She refers to it as her punk phase, but it was really just the hair."

"Wow! And what phase were you going through? Were you some kind of hippie or something?"

"No, I'm afraid I looked pretty much the same, just younger," he said. "Now, why don't you go upstairs and get some sleep? But do me a favor and don't tell your brother. About your mom and me, I mean. I don't want to worry Carter over something that'll all work out in the end."

Max made her way back to bed, but she didn't close her eyes until she'd heard her father's footsteps crossing the hall and the sound of his own bedroom door closing. Even then, as she finally felt sleep creeping in on the edges of her consciousness, she fought it for a while longer.

Alone, Max whispered something aloud. There were no stars to wish upon in that foreign room so far, far away from home, so she wished upon the dark instead. It was an awkward wish, all tangled up with worries about her parents' marriage and her brother and how Max herself was getting older. Everything in her life felt twisted together and impossible to pull apart, like a knot of pink hair.

Just make it all better, she wished. The dark, of course, didn't answer back. But something heard.

CHAPTER SIX

"Here's where they came in," said the ratcatcher. Patrick. Or maybe he'd said his name was Peter. Max couldn't remember.

Whatever his name, he was a ratcatcher, or *pest control professional,* as he'd corrected Carter when Max's brother had answered the front door shouting, "Dad! The ratcatcher's here!"

The ratcatcher introduced himself in nearly perfect English, and with a smile on his face, like he was in on the joke of how ridiculous his job title really was, so that was a point in his favor. Still, Max didn't care for him. Maybe it was the way he instantly dismissed the number of rats they'd claimed to have seen. He'd nodded as they described the swarm of rodents pouring out of the vent, but they might as well have been telling him about a beanstalk growing up to the sky. Or maybe Max didn't like him because she'd dreamed all night about rats and pipers and missing children, and maybe he was just unlucky enough to be a part of all that in her head.

Or maybe it was something else. Maybe it was a feeling in her gut.

Regardless, the ratcatcher was now shining his flashlight into a hole half the size of Carter in the cellar wall. Beyond was darkness and an odd, sweet-smelling breeze. The edges of the hole looked chewed on.

"They're taking the insulation," he said, pointing to the cottony yellow stuff lying in clumps near the hole. "They love this stuff. Makes for cozy nests."

"How did no one notice something like that?" asked their father. The night's sleep had helped, and the bags under his eyes looked a little less like bruises. "And where's that breeze coming from?"

"I'm sure there's another hole at the other end of this one that leads outside. Here. Take a listen."

Very faintly, Max could hear music drifting up through the hole. She looked over at Carter. "Weird," he whispered.

"Someone's got their stereo up too loud," said the ratcatcher, laughing. "This tunnel probably goes under the house next door. Just a few of them can chew through plaster, even metal wire, in no time. Wouldn't take them long to do this."

"A few?" said Max. "There were hundreds!"

The ratcatcher smiled at her. "I'm sure it seemed that way at the time."

"No, she's right," said Carter. "Thousands even."

"I've been doing this job for many years, and I can tell

you I've never seen a home infestation that big. Train tunnels and sewers, maybe, but not homes."

"They didn't imagine it," said their father. "You saw the tracks in the kitchen."

"I'm not saying there weren't a lot of them," said the ratcatcher, holding up his hands in mock surrender. "And to be honest, it doesn't matter. The course of treatment will be the same whether it's one rat or a hundred."

"And just what is the treatment?" asked their father. "I'm not sure we should stay here tonight if you're using rat poisons. All those chemicals."

The ratcatcher scratched his chin. The man was totally nondescript, with the kind of face you couldn't pick out of a crowd if you tried. And he was awfully clean-cut for someone who spent his days crawling around people's basements.

"Well, there are options," he said. "Why don't we go upstairs and look over the paperwork. Your landlord will be paying, of course, but since you're the tenant, I'll still need your signature."

When they got to the kitchen, their father put on a pot of coffee as the ratcatcher sat down at the table. The music was louder up here, coming in through the open kitchen window.

"At least it's classical," the ratcatcher said. "Can't stand pop songs today." He was rummaging through his shoulder bag.

"So, where's your mother?" he asked Max as she sat down opposite him.

"She's back in the States," Max said, not that it was any of the man's business.

"It's a shame about them."

Max looked at him. Had she just heard him right?

"What did you just say?"

"Hmm? Me? Nothing."

At that moment, Max's father reappeared with the coffee. "Milk or sugar?"

"Black's fine for me," the ratcatcher said.

"I'm sorry," said their father. "But could you tell me your name again? I'm bad with names."

"Oh, please don't apologize," he said, blowing on his coffee.

Then he told them his name again, and this time Max repeated it to herself so she wouldn't forget. It was Harold. Or Hans. Maybe it was something longer? Why couldn't she remember? She couldn't have slept that well if she was this tired. If she forgot the name of someone literally seconds after hearing it, she really was brain-dead.

Soon, however, her father and ratcatcher what's-his-name were busy going over a checklist of remedies for their pest problem. Traps first, the ratcatcher recommended, and if that didn't work, he'd find them where they lived. Not that it was the Weber family's problem anymore. In a few days they would be on a plane back home. Her father had promised.

Carter was hanging back, kind of watching it all with a look of concentration on his face. He was probably somewhere in his own head, daydreaming, as usual.

Max walked over to him and mock-punched him in the arm.

"You hit like a girl," he said.

"So what do you think of all this?"

"Seems to know what he's doing," said Carter. Then he whispered, "I wonder how someone becomes a ratcatch—um, I mean, pest control professional, anyway. When do you decide to do that?"

Max leaned up against the wall next to her brother. "I don't think it's popular on career day at school."

Carter smiled. "No way."

"Hey, what did he say his name was?" asked Max. "I keep forgetting."

"Oh, it's . . . it's . . ." Carter scrunched up his nose like he was smelling something rotten. "I can't remember. That's weird."

Max got that feeling again, the one she'd gotten yesterday when she'd lost track of Carter after the play, the feeling she'd had when she'd seen the man standing in the shadows. It was a prickle at the base of her neck, a queasiness in her stomach that told her something was not right. Why couldn't Carter remember the ratcatcher's name, either?

"What's up?" asked Carter. "You don't look good."

"Do me a favor," said Max. "Go wait upstairs."

"Huh?"

"Just do it!" she snapped.

Their father finished signing the ratcatcher's contract. The two were shaking hands as Max approached.

"Here's your copy, in English," the ratcatcher was saying. "And, like I said, don't worry about the fine print. Formalities."

"I understand," said Max's father. "So, when can you start?"

"Let me run out to my van to get something." He smiled at them. "Don't anyone go away!"

Her father gave a polite chuckle, and Max just watched as the ratcatcher left through the front door.

"Odd fellow," said her father, letting out a long sigh. "But I think we'll all sleep better tonight once this is taken care of. Though I haven't ruled out going to a hotel."

Through the front door window, Max could see the rat-catcher opening the door to his van. It was a plain white vehicle. No company name or logo.

"Dad," Max asked. "Did you catch his name?"

"Hmm? Oh, it's . . . Darn it, he told me twice. . . . It's on the tip of my tongue!"

That sealed it. Three of them and not one could remember his name. And there was the unmarked van. No logo. The music grew louder. It no longer sounded far off; it was right here with her. The room felt like it was tipping beneath her feet.

Max snatched the contract from the table. It was mostly legalese, but she couldn't find a name anywhere. She flipped the page over. On the back was a single sentence, but unlike the typed front page, this was handwritten in a cursive, flowing font:

In signing I hereby offer as tender my children, blood of my blood, the last of their line, in payment to the Piper, and the deal is done.

The fine print. Max's breath caught in her throat. A scream that wouldn't come out. She turned to see the ratcatcher bounding up the front steps to the porch, two at a time.

"Dad!" she screamed. "Lock the door! Don't let him back in!"

But it was too late. The door flew open, and . . .

The music soared. Her father was saying something, calling worriedly to Max, but it sounded as if he were talking under water. Max was dreaming, and nothing could hurt you in a dream. She could feel Carter's hand tugging on her sleeve, and she felt a slight twinge of annoyance that her brother was still in the dream with her; why hadn't he gone upstairs like she'd told him to? But that didn't really matter. None of it mattered anymore. All she could care about was the song, the longing and sadness in the music that made her heart want to burst.

Then Max was looking at herself in a tall mirror. It was an old thing, with gilded edges that had tarnished over time. A hairline crack split down the center of the looking glass and it distorted her reflection so that she looked like two halves of a person stuck awkwardly together. A girl and a young woman, yet neither one looked right on her own. Max didn't know how to stitch them into one, but if she followed the dream music, she wouldn't have to.

Then Max was dancing toward a far-off place, a land of summer and trees and flowers so bright it was like staring into the sun, and she didn't care if she ever, ever came home again.

PART II

NEW HAMELIN

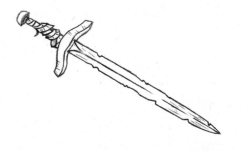

Lukas was dreaming of the man and the woman again. The woman held him, and in her arms Lukas was smaller and still soft with milk fat. He couldn't see her face this time. In some dreams she had a face, but it often changed, and Lukas never knew which one was true. The man was talking to him, lecturing him about not shirking his duties at the gate wall. Lukas didn't want to hear it, so he snuggled closer to the woman, burying his head in her chest, where he felt safe. Comforted.

When the dream was interrupted by the ringing of a tower bell, Lukas awoke in a panic. The gate! Had he forgotten the gate wall, overslept his shift? But bright yellow daylight was streaming in through the shutters of his small room. He'd already done his shift, a full watch last evening. Across from Lukas, Finn's bed was empty, which meant that the other boy was already at the gate. That meant it was the day watch.

Then why was the tower bell ringing?

Alarm settled to annoyance as Lukas counted the rings of the bell. Three, then a pause, and three again. Scouts were returning with something that needed his attention, but it wasn't a village-wide alarm. They weren't under attack.

Still, he was being summoned and there would be no going back to bed. As Lukas stood up, he nearly doubled over from the crick in his neck. He really needed to restuff his mattress, but there was precious little furry moss available in the village these days. Finn had sent out a foraging party, but furry moss wouldn't be high on their list of priorities. Maybe he'd see if the girls had any to spare—Emilie owed him one favor, at least.

He'd been so exhausted when he'd come off his watch that he'd collapsed onto the bed without taking off his clothes, so he needn't bother dressing. He slipped on his hard leather shoes and wrapped the pigskin leggings up tight. It was a routine he'd gotten used to, and he only paused before belting on the sword. It still didn't feel right wearing that thing on his hip. The Sword of the Eldest Boy was solid black iron, warped and dented in places, but it was a far superior weapon than any other in the village. No studded club for him, or spear. The sword was the weapon of the Captain of the Watch, and it had belonged to Leon, and to Marc before him. They'd each been Eldest Boy, before they were lost. All they'd left behind was the sword, and regardless of how it felt, or how little he wanted it, the sword belonged to Lukas. He was Eldest Boy, now.

Lukas stepped out of the west barracks and squinted up at the sky. It was still early morning, and he'd only been asleep for a few hours, yet the village of New Hamelin was already well into its daily business. He could smell bread baking, and he watched as a pair of middle boys argued over who had spilled their buckets of river water. Lukas shook his head. It didn't matter who spilled them. There were too many things to do. There were always things to do.

He took a slight detour on his way to the gate and crossed the village square. There was a strong summer breeze this morning, but while it might come as a relief to the children working in the gardens, any unusually cool breeze was reason for concern when you were Captain of the Watch. The Summer Tree stood tall and proud in the middle of the square, and little ones played beneath its sheltering boughs. Lukas paused just long enough to examine the tree's leaves. Most were still a lush green, but he spotted yellow in among them, turning fast before his eyes. Wind ruffled the branches. No breeze anymore, this was a strong gust now, and other children were noticing the sudden drop in temperature. They turned to Lukas with anxious looks.

Is this an autumn wind? their worried faces asked. *Is winter coming tonight? Is darkness coming tonight?*

Lukas stepped up his pace as he made for the main gate. Here on the Summer Isle, warmth and sunlight reigned. The nights rarely grew dark, as twilight lasted from dusk until dawn. But every now and then a chill wind would start to blow and bring with it a sudden change. The temperatures would plummet, and that night a full moon would rise—a Winter's Moon—and chase away the warmth. True night would descend, a dark winter that lasted one night only. But one night was enough, because things crept out of the dark on nights like that, things that shunned the light. Dangerous things.

The wind was blowing. The leaves were turning on the Summer Tree. These were bad signs.

As he neared the gate, Lukas heard someone call his name, and he looked up to see Paul running his way. The smaller boy had a gang of middles trailing him. He always had three or four of them hanging around anywhere he went, ready to help him get into whatever spot of mischief he had planned for the day. Though he was an elder and an excellent scout, Paul was a born troublemaker. Most of the time his jests were harmless, but every now and again he would push it too far, and most recently he'd caught and jarred a kobold. He'd obviously intended it as some sort of joke, hoping to use it to spoil someone's milk or force it to teach him a charm or two. But if he'd actually managed to smuggle the little creature in, it could have been disastrous for the entire village. Such a thing was strictly forbidden— none but New Hameliners were allowed inside. Not even the Peddler was allowed in. No exceptions.

Paul had been taken off scouting duty after that and confined to the village. He would not be allowed to venture beyond the gate until Emilie relented. Really, she was just asking for more trouble, as the worst thing you could do was to shut Paul in, but Emilie was Eldest Girl and once she had made up her mind, there was no changing it.

"What is it, Paul?" Lukas asked as the shorter boy caught up with him. "I'm on my way to the gate. Didn't you hear the bell?"

"Sure, I heard it," said Paul. "But I have something very

important to show you and it can't wait. Something I invented!" The boy was holding a pig's bladder in his hands. It looked full.

"Are you trying to tell me that you created a water skin? Because we have enough of those already."

"Of course I didn't invent the water skin," said Paul. "But I have invented a new use for it. Watch!" At once, Paul clutched his stomach and began to moan. He bent over as if in pain, and for a second Lukas considered calling for help. But then again, this was Paul.

"Ah, my gut!" moaned the boy. "Too many figs with breakfast . . . feel that I might . . ."

Then he let out a loud, ripping fart. Or at least it sounded like a fart. Lukas saw that Paul had stuck the bladder full of air beneath his arm and squeezed it, making a pitch-perfect farting sound. The children around him burst into laughter.

Lukas couldn't help but smile himself. It really did sound like a fart.

Paul stood up and took a bow. "Do you know what I'm going to do?" he asked Lukas with a wink. "I'm going to slip this under Emilie's chair cushion before the next meeting of the Elders! Can you imagine their faces when the Eldest Girl lets out an enormous fart just as she's calling the meeting to order?"

That would be a sight to see. But Lukas wouldn't want to cross Emilie. The girl could make Paul's life hell for years to come. Longer, even. "I don't think that's a good idea, Paul."

"Ah, what fun are you, *Eldest Boy?*"

Lukas scowled at the title, but then the wind picked up again, and this time there was no denying the chill. Paul had felt it, too, and the wry grin melted from the boy's face. "It's getting colder, isn't it?"

"I think so," said Lukas. "And the Summer Tree's yellowing."

"It'll be tonight or tomorrow at the latest, then," said Paul. "Check the forest to be sure."

"Finn's at the gate," said Lukas. "I'm on my way there now."

"You'll have your hands full," said Paul. "Any chance Emilie will let me have my bow back? I could be of use."

"I'm afraid not."

"Well then," sighed Paul. "There's only one thing for it. Emilie gets the fart bag!"

With that, Paul turned and marched off, his little group of middles nipping at his heels like a pack of wolf cubs. Paul was going to be a problem so long as Emilie kept him cooped up. Leon would have known how to keep the boy out of trouble, but Lukas wasn't Leon. Or Marc. It wasn't long ago that Lukas would have chased after Paul, laughing along with the rest. He might actually have helped Paul do his mischief.

But Lukas had responsibilities now, the same ones the man in his dream had been lecturing him about. Eldest Boy. Captain of the Watch. Lukas tried to shake it away. Dreams could be dangerous on the Summer Isle. Dreams led you astray.

Lukas's mood had only grown more sour by the time he reached the gate, and he didn't bother to hide his scowl as the other boys of the Watch saluted him. He climbed the tall ladder to the south tower bell, which looked out over the gate wall that encircled their entire village. Its foundation was mostly piled stones, but the wall's sturdy timbers were dug deep into the earth and reached thirty feet high, topped with a fence of thorn-wood branches ringed by a walking platform. From up there, the Watch could see for miles. Beyond the gate, the Peddler's Road snaked past New Hamelin into the Shimmering Forest, where, even at midday, floating lights could be seen in the shade, blinking like wreaths of twinkling stars. A beautiful place, but dangerous for the unwary. As dangerous as any place outside the village, but nice enough to look at when one needed to pass the long hours on duty. To the north, treacherous mountains loomed over everything. The Peddler's Road stretched even that far, though no one other than the Peddler himself walked it. Gnomes used to come down from the mountains to trade ore for the village's woodcrafts, but that was long ago.

Travelers of any kind were uncommon these days, except for the Peddler. The wilds had grown too perilous for anyone else.

Lukas found Finn waiting for him atop the tower. It was cramped inside, and Lukas had to bend his head or else crack it against the low ceiling. "Took you long enough," said Finn as Lukas joined him at the window. "Dreaming of Emilie, perhaps?"

"Bite your tongue off!" said Lukas. "Unless you want to conjure me more nightmares."

The bell ringer on duty was a small, red-faced boy named Pidge, and though the boy pretended not to hear what his elders were saying, Lukas could feel his own ears getting red with embarrassment. He needed to change the conversation away from Emilie, and quickly.

"So what did you haul me out of bed for?" Lukas asked, though he feared he knew the answer.

"There," answered Finn, his face growing serious. He gestured to the Shimmering Forest, where patches of yellow were evident among the green trees and were spreading. The leaves of the forest were already turning. By afternoon the forest would be a sea of orange and gold, and by evening those branches would be bare.

"It'll be tonight, then," said Lukas. "What's the status of your scouts?"

"The last team is coming up the road now," said Finn, and he pointed to a few distant shapes approaching.

"John's foraging team back already? I'm glad, but I didn't expect them this soon. Not without Paul scouting the way for them."

"They're early."

Lukas wasn't upset that the scouts were ahead of schedule. Finn would want his boys to stay out as long as was possible because scouts were a prideful lot, almost to the point of being boastful. But Lukas was Eldest Boy now and Captain. Like it or not, he was responsible for the safety of the entire village, which meant that tonight everyone stayed inside the walls. When the Winter's Moon was in the sky, the gates opened for no one.

Because if *they* got inside, the whole village would be lost.

"John sent a runner ahead to warn us," said Finn. "He's down at the gate, getting watered."

"Warn us?" said Lukas. "Warn us about what?"

"That's the other reason I had Pidge ring the bell for you," answered Finn. "I would've let you get a few hours of sleep at least, but John's team isn't coming back alone. They found someone."

Incredulous, Lukas stared at his friend. "What? More kobolds? He's as bad as Paul! Everyone knows the rules, and if Emilie catches wind—"

"Not kobolds," interrupted Finn.

Lukas paused. "Not elves, surely."

"Not elves, either," said Finn. "Children. Lukas, they've found two children."

Lukas opened his mouth, only to close it again. What was there to say? Children. How long had it been? How long had it been since Lukas had laid eyes on a child not of New Hamelin? How many hundreds of years?

❧ CHAPTER EIGHT ❧

Carter had been dreaming of pancakes. Which was odd, because he didn't really care for pancakes. He liked the things you put on top of pancakes—the syrup, strawberries and whipped cream. But he could do without the pancake itself. Something about the texture was just wrong. Yet, in his dream he couldn't get enough, the doughier the better.

When he finally woke up from the pancake dream and saw that there were no real pancakes in front of him, he was very disappointed until he remembered he didn't like pancakes. Then his disappointment turned to something closer to fear.

Carter was alone in a tiny wooden room. Not like the wooden room he slept in back at home, plastered over with drywall and paint, but a real wooden room. Made of logs. Like a log cabin, yes, that was what he was in. Or more like a shed, actually. He was lying on the floor on some kind of pallet made of straw, inside a shed made of logs, with no pancakes and no idea how he'd gotten there.

He sat up and examined his surroundings. A stool in the corner held some kind of lamp. It looked like a candle mounted inside a hollowed-out gourd. Through cracks in the wall he could see a gray day outside, and he hugged his arms around himself as he shivered—it was cold enough to see his breath in front of his face. The last thing Carter remembered was his sister shouting something about locking the front door, but hadn't that been part of the dream, too? And he remembered music, music that promised trees and light and gently flowing streams and warm summer air. Happiness.

And pancakes.

There was a sound outside, and Carter stood up as the door slowly opened. It alarmed him at first, but he felt a small touch of relief when he saw a boy walk in. He was not much older than Carter's sister, but he was dressed in a strange mix-match of rough cloth and leather, like he'd walked out of a Renaissance fair. An ugly black sword was strapped to his hip. Carter didn't like the look of that, but at least the boy was smiling.

"Are you thirsty?" the boy asked, holding out a water skin.

"Okay," said Carter, warily. He was terribly thirsty. The water tasted like leather, but it quenched his thirst.

"I'm Lukas," said the boy.

"Carter."

"Are you a ghost?" asked Lukas.

"Wow, I hope not," said Carter. "Um, can you tell me where I am?"

"You're in our village. Our scouts found you asleep on a bed of wild furry moss, on the edge of the Shimmering Forest. They tried to wake you, but when you didn't stir they brought you back here. You slept the whole afternoon away and only just now awoke."

"Uh, I don't know what any of that meant, but, I suppose . . . thanks?"

Lukas studied Carter for a moment. "You don't know the Shimmering Forest?"

Carter shook his head.

"Then where did you come from? The mountains?"

"New York, originally. But my family and I were traveling abroad."

"Your clothes are strange."

"I was going to say the same about you. No offense."

Lukas almost laughed, Carter could tell, but had caught himself. Lukas slung a pack off his shoulder and set it down on the little stool with a thud. As he untied the drawstrings, Carter began to worry again. What was inside that bag? All at once, every movie he'd ever seen where a prisoner was tortured came to mind. Make them feel comfortable, then surprise them with pain. That was how they did it. Good cop, bad cop.

"What's that?" Carter asked, taking a step backward.

"You should know," said Lukas, his voice taking on a strangely formal tone, "that I am the Eldest Boy, Captain of the Watch. If you are a wicked spirit in disguise, now's your chance to confess it."

"If I'm a what?"

"It will go easier on you if you do."

"I don't know what you are talking about," said Carter. He was sweating now. They were going to torture him, ask him questions about spirits, and he had no answers to give. He didn't even know what was going on.

Lukas opened the bag and produced . . . a cowbell. It was crudely shaped and looked like someone's failed shop-class project, but it was definitely a cowbell.

"What are you going to do with—" But before he could finish, Lukas began clanging the bell in Carter's face. *Bong! Bong! Bong!*

"Hey!" cried Carter. "Cut it out!"

"It pains you?" Lukas asked.

"It's super annoying! You want me to bang that thing next to your ear and see how you like it?"

This time, Lukas didn't bother holding in his laughter.

"Yes, it is a bothersome sound," he said. "But evil spirits cannot abide the ringing of bells, nor cold iron. It causes them unimaginable pain. And well, I'm sorry, but we had to be sure."

"You had to be sure I'm not a spirit?" said Carter.

Lukas set the bell down on the table and studied Carter. "I had a friend like you once," he said after a moment. "He was lame, too."

Carter felt his cheeks redden. *Lame* was not a word that Carter liked. He was not lame in any way. But Lukas's expression as he said the word remained open, friendly. The boy didn't seem to mean it as an insult.

"Did you injure your leg in an accident?" asked Lukas.

"No, I was born like this," said Carter. This, at least, was familiar territory. He was used to having to explain himself to people. Everyone wanted to know; it was just a matter of when they worked up the courage to ask. "I'm club-footed, which means my foot bends out the wrong way. It's a condition that usually gets better with treatment or surgery. *Usually.* Guess I'm just unusual."

"The thing you wear on your foot . . ."

"It's a brace."

"I've never seen anything like it," said Lukas. "It's a tool that helps you walk?"

Carter nodded. "Sorta."

"Does it hurt?"

"Not really," said Carter. "You get used to it."

"You can move around much better with it than my friend could," said Lukas. "All Timm had was a simple wooden crutch."

Carter nodded, and tried to smile. He was starting to suspect that this Lukas kid might be cracked in the head. Or maybe Carter had been kidnapped by some kind of insane cult. Maybe they stole kids away as a recruitment strategy and brainwashed them into working in Renaissance fairs for the rest of their lives.

Thinking of kids reminded Carter of someone. "Um, when you found me in the . . . fuzzy glen or whatever. Did you see my sister there, too?"

At the mention of Carter's sister, Lukas's expression grew worried. "She's your sister?" he asked. Carter nodded.

"Then we need to hurry," said Lukas. "Her situation is worse than yours. She's in danger."

"Danger?" said Carter, suddenly alarmed. He'd been in here listening to cowbells while Max was in trouble?

"People here think her an ill omen."

"An ill omen? She's a pain, but she's not any kind of omen. She's just my sister."

Lukas shook his head. "There are queer things about her, but it's not just that. She woke before you and . . . she kicked one of the Watch between the legs."

That sounded like Max.

"And she wears very sturdy shoes," added Lukas.

Definitely Max.

"We have to hurry," said Lukas, opening the door. "Daylight is fading, and they will decide soon whether or not to put her outside the gate."

"What gate?" asked Carter, following him. "What's that mean?"

"It means that if she's put outside the gate, she'll likely die."

CHAPTER NINE

Max was being led through a village of children. There were a few her age, like the boys who were urging her on by spear point, but most were younger. Some looked as young as four or five, hiding behind the skirts of older girls. In this entire village of dirt streets and ramshackle cottages, Max couldn't see a single adult. Every face that peered out at her from a window or a doorway belonged to a child. The looks on those faces ranged from curiosity to fear, or were maybe a mixture of both. She supposed she deserved some of it, especially from the leader of the boys pushing her along. She'd reacted hastily when she'd awoken to find him looking down at her, and perhaps kicking him had been a bad introduction.

As they went, Max tried to make a mental map of where she was being led, but the layout of this little village was so haphazard and illogical, she couldn't tell which way was which. Cottages were crammed up against one another in odd configurations. The structures appeared solidly built, but everywhere she looked there were little touches that served no real purpose: a rope bridge connecting two neighboring windows when it would have been easy enough to simply walk across the street; a house with no door on the first floor, only ladders going up. This was a town dreamed up by children.

Not that it was simply one big playground, far from it. There were well-tended vegetable gardens here and there, and from the smell, Max guessed that livestock were kept nearby. And then there was the wall that fenced it all in. It had to have been thirty feet high, and it circled the entire village. There was nothing whimsical about that structure. A ledge ran along the entire wall, and boys with spears patroled up there. At each corner of the wall stood a tall tower—for lookouts, Max supposed—and while Max watched, a boy leaned out of one of the towers and chased away a few crows who'd been perched up there watching Max's march through the village.

The sky was gray and getting darker, and in the short time she'd been awake, it'd grown noticeably colder. She was already wishing she had more than just her T-shirt, but she didn't think now was the best time to ask someone to borrow a jacket. Head held high, Max let herself be escorted through this strange, almost unbelievable, village while doing her very best not to let on just how scared she really was.

They passed through a small square built around a single enormous tree. The ground beneath it was covered with fallen autumn leaves, and the branches were bare. Boys with long torches lit tall hanging lanterns spaced out every few yards, and in every window burned a candle. Max couldn't understand why they would need so many lanterns, but she didn't think it wise to ask more questions just yet. At last they stopped at a cabin on the outskirts of the village, near that imposing wall of theirs. The door to the cabin opened and out walked her brother.

"Carter!" Max shouted, and the two of them grabbed each other in a giant hug.

"Do you know what's going on?" Max whispered. "What is this place, and who are these people?"

"Isn't it awesome?" Carter answered. "Don't worry, they're friendly."

Awesome? Max glanced back at the scowling faces of the boys who had "escorted" her here. They didn't look friendly.

"I heard you kicked one of them," said Carter. *Well, there was that.*

"Are you sure you're okay?"

"He's fine," said another boy, stepping up behind him. Instead of holding a spear, this one had a sword belted at his waist. But he wore a friendly grin. "I'm Lukas," he said.

"He's the Captain of the Watch," said Carter, impressed.

"He's what?" asked Max.

"There is little time to explain," said Lukas. "I've talked to the Eldest Girl and she's agreed to let you and your brother stay the night, but you'll be confined inside here."

"Confined? So we're prisoners?"

"Max," said Carter. "It was either that or we'd be sent outside the walls."

"So?" said Max, her voice rising. None of this made

sense, and no one was bothering to explain anything to her. Surely this was a bad dream that wouldn't end. "What if I want to be outside? What's so bad out there, anyway?"

Lukas shook his head. "Your brother asked the same thing. There's too much to explain now. You'll be safe within the village walls, but the outside is dangerous. Especially tonight."

"Safe *where?*" shouted Max. "I still don't know where we are!"

"This is the Summer Isle," said Lukas, but his smile had disappeared and his voice turned thick with bitterness. "Welcome to the village of New Hamelin."

Max didn't understand. Had she heard him right? *Hamelin?* This wasn't any Hamelin that she recognized.

"Max, please," said Carter. "I think we can trust them."

"It's only until dawn," said Lukas. "At first light, Emilie will want to speak to you, and we'll have time to explain everything. You have questions for us, but I believe we have even more for you."

Max looked at her brother, then at the stony faces of the guards. "Fine," she said.

"There are two beds and blankets," said Lukas, leading them inside. It was a small room with no windows.

"Thanks," said Carter. "I'm sure we'll be comfy."

Lukas looked out the doorway, at the sky. It was almost dark. "I have to go," said Lukas. "But promise me you'll both stay inside tonight, no matter what."

"Well, since you're obviously going to lock us in, I don't think we'll have much of a choice, will we?" said Max.

"You don't understand. There are locks on both sides of

this door," said Lukas. "I will lock it from the outside, and I want you to bolt it shut from the inside as well."

Max examined the door. Sure enough, there was a sturdy wooden dead bolt on the inside. "That doesn't make sense. Why lock a door on both sides?"

"Just promise me," said Lukas. "I'll be back at dawn to fetch you, but this door is to stay shut and locked until then. Understand?"

Carter nodded and Max glared, but she felt certain they were both thinking the same thing—*something bad was going to happen out there tonight.*

"There are extra blankets," said Lukas, and he set a small lantern on the table near the beds. "Keep the lantern lit at all times. *Don't let it go out.* It's filled with rendered pig's fat, so it smells foul but burns well enough. Careful with it, though."

Lukas closed and locked the door, and from outside he called, "I'll be back for you at sunrise. Try to sleep."

Max and Carter were left in that windowless cabin with only the little lantern to keep them company until dawn. They unfolded the blankets and pulled them tightly around themselves, shivering against the chill. Max wished they had a fire, but there was no fireplace and no chimney, no portal to the outside at all, save the door.

"Carter, do you have any idea what's going on?"

Her brother shook his head. "Not really. I thought I was dreaming, but now I don't think so."

"Me too," said Max. She'd been trying to piece together the last things she remembered, but they were fuzzy, distant. "Do you remember the ratcatcher?"

Carter nodded. "Although I was hoping he was a dream, too."

"And music?"

"Uh-huh."

"Well, at least I'm not crazy," said Max. "Or I am, and you are, too."

"That's reassuring."

"That's what big sisters are for."

Carter smiled, but he shivered as he pulled his blanket tighter around him. Max could hear his teeth chattering.

"Why don't you sit here on my bed with me," said Max. "We can keep each other warm, at least."

Carter sat next to her on the bed, and they threw both blankets over them. "Hey, remember when we used to make forts out of blankets?" asked Carter.

"Yeah," said Max. "And the same rules apply, no farting under the covers."

"You know, Max, you can stop trying to make me laugh. I'm okay; I'm not scared."

Carter scooted closer for warmth, and Max put her arm around him. "Okay," said Max, and they sat together for a while in silence, as the little sunlight they could see through the cracks in their cabin faded. They would occasionally hear voices outside their door as children ran past and the older boys ordered them to get indoors. But soon enough the sun set entirely and the only light was their little lamp, and the only sounds were the sounds of the wind howling in the night. The village was bracing itself, bracing itself for something bad.

I'm glad you're not scared, Carter, thought Max. *Because I'm terrified.*

❧ CHAPTER TEN ❧

L ukas bounded along the walkway after Finn, mindful
of the steep drop. A slick frost had already formed in
places, but he'd been a member of the Watch long before becoming Eldest Boy. Finn might have been naturally
quicker on his feet, but Lukas knew every splinter of the
gate wall.

The first sighting had come just after sundown, near the
front gate. Only shadows in the dark, and they'd fled as the
Watch shot a few flaming arrows in their direction. After
that, all had been quiet as the pale Winter's Moon rose in
the sky. With that moon, winter and darkness fell across the
land—a rare thing on the Summer Isle. But it was a winter
that would last one night only. With dawn, spring would
come again, and it was the Watch's job to ensure that they
all stayed alive long enough to enjoy it.

The second sighting came just before midnight. As the

alarm bell rang out from the northeastern tower, Lukas could already see torches moving through the streets and along the gate wall as members of the Watch answered the bell ringer's call. Perhaps it was just more shadows, testing them, probing New Hamelin's defenses. Perhaps not.

Finn, however, told Lukas he was needed elsewhere and pulled him in the opposite direction, to the southeastern tower instead. No bells were ringing here, but Lukas found two members of the Watch waiting for him on the walkway. One of them cradled an unconscious boy in his arms.

"It's Pidge," said Finn. "The bell ringer."

"Tell me what happened."

"We found him like this when we were doing our rounds," said one of the boys. "Got a nasty cut on his head. We told Finn and he ran to get you."

Lukas knelt beside the unconscious boy. He'd seen Pidge just yesterday on day duty, but now the usually ruddy-cheeked boy's face was sickly white and his hair slick with blood that looked black in the moonlight.

"He must've fallen from his tower," said one of the boys. "Slipped on the frost."

"Not likely," answered Finn. "Pidge knows his job too well."

Lukas stared up at the tall ladder that climbed from the walkway to the bell tower. The tower was a dark spire in the night that reached a full fifteen feet higher than the wall.

"Anyone know what's happening over at the northeastern tower?" asked Lukas. "Why are the bells ringing?"

"A few of them tried the north wall," said one of the boys. "But they mustn't have tried very hard."

"We had a possible sighting at the front gate earlier, too," said Lukas.

"Looks like it's our lucky night," said Finn wryly.

"Not for Pidge," said Lukas. "He needs Emilie's medicines. You'll likely find her in the village hall, telling stories to those who can't sleep. Can you and the boys carry him there?"

Finn nodded. "Of course."

"Has someone searched Pidge's bell tower already?" asked Lukas.

Finn opened his mouth to answer, then paused. He looked like someone who'd forgotten his pants. "No."

"We were all busy looking after Pidge," said one of the boys quickly.

Lukas stood and peered up at the tower. Its windows were all dark. "Someone's put the lantern out," said Lukas softly. The other boys exchanged looks. If Pidge had fallen, he wouldn't have stopped to douse his lantern first.

What would Leon have done if he were here? He would have tended to Pidge and sent the boys up top to search the tower. The Eldest Boy's job was to give orders, to lead. Leon would have had nothing to prove by rushing into danger alone.

"I'll go up," said Finn.

But Lukas wasn't Leon. "No, you get Pidge out of here. Give me your torch."

Finn started to protest, but a look from Lukas silenced him. Then Lukas took the torch in hand and, without another word, started climbing the bell tower ladder. It was tricky business climbing one-handed, but he dare not drop the torch, because it would be pitch dark inside that tower with the lantern out. And he'd have little enough room inside to move around. Bell ringers were always middles, because the middle boys were generally smaller and the towers weren't spacious. And because it was usually safer to be a lookout in a bell tower than a guard on the gate wall. Usually.

Lukas paused just underneath the trapdoor. The hatch was open, and his torch illuminated the interior room above him enough so that he could see his torch's flickering firelight dancing on the low ceiling. But that didn't mean there wasn't something hiding just out of sight.

The Watch had a saying—*If you don't fear the dark, the dark will fear you.* On nights like this, the darkness fed on your fears and spat them back at you. So every boy of the Watch worked hard to clear his mind of such things, and in the end every boy failed. Lukas had always hated that saying, because he knew that any person who didn't feel afraid now and again wasn't a proper person at all. It was how you faced your fear that made you a boy of the Watch.

Lukas swallowed the bitter taste in his mouth and took a deep breath, trying to calm his racing heart. Then he raised himself through the hatch, into the lightless bell tower.

He moved quickly, ready to strike out with the torch at anything that moved, but nothing did. The tower was empty. The bell, an iron-banded ringer bigger than Lukas's fist, hung silently from the ceiling, and Pidge's darkened lantern rested on the floor. The tower had open windows on all sides, allowing a bell ringer to keep watch in every direction. Below, the village was aglow with hanging lights and window candles—the lamplighters had done their job well.

Lukas hoped everyone down there was being cautious, however, because an accidental fire would be just as dangerous a threat as what lay outside the walls. Yet another concern for the Eldest Boy.

Beyond the wall, the moon hung pale in the sky, but did nothing to lessen the dark. Lukas touched his fingers to Pidge's lantern. It was still warm, so someone had recently put it out. Perhaps Pidge *had* extinguished it before leaving his post?

Then Lukas detected a sound, just a small sound like the creak of a board underfoot, but it hadn't come from the floor. It had come from the ceiling. Lukas looked up, afraid to breathe, afraid of the noise his own breath might make.

There it was again. And again. Something was walking, or crawling, across the tower roof. He could track its movement by the give in the boards as it crossed to the other side. Whatever it was, it was big. When it reached the edge, Lukas heard sniffing and scraping as a moonlit silhouette dropped down from the roof and into the open window.

A long snout sniffed the air. Red eyes reflected Lukas's torchlight. The creature's fur was dark and bristly, and it wore a leather strap stuffed with knives across its chest like a bandolier. Roughly man-shaped, it was a big creature, and standing upright, it would have been at least a foot taller than Lukas.

It was one of the largest rats he'd ever seen, and it had somehow gotten over the wall.

Pidge hadn't slipped; he had been pushed. There wasn't space in the cramped tower room to draw his sword, so he brought up his torch in a two-handed defensive stance and readied himself. Rats hated fire, at least, so that was something.

The rat leaned in through the tower window and sniffed again. Its beady eyes settled on Lukas and the torch as it let out a low growl. Then, in one swift, unexpected motion, the rat turned and leaped away from the tall tower. Lukas dashed to the window in pursuit, but he was too late. He peered into the darkness, searching for any sign of the creature below, but all he could see were the faint outlines of cottages, the glow of candles behind shuttered windows where children slept soundly in their beds, sure that the Watch would keep them safe.

But tonight the Watch had failed. Lukas had failed. A rat was loose in New Hamelin.

CHAPTER ELEVEN

Panicked cries rose from somewhere nearby, waking Carter from a dreamless sleep. Someone was shouting. "What's happening out there?" he asked.

"Shush," said Max with her finger to her lips. She mouthed the word *listen*. Max was staring at the cabin door.

Carter's heartbeats kept pace with the seconds until he heard it, too. A closer sound than the distant voices, like a scraping of wood across wood, like the sliding of a bolt.

The door. Someone was opening it from the outside, opening the door they had forgotten to lock.

The handle turned as Carter lunged across the room. He stumbled a little on his leg and grimaced in pain, but he managed to grab the door handle with both hands as he fell, yanking it back closed. For a second or two, it stayed that way, but then whatever was on the other side pulled again. It was strong, far stronger than a ten-year-old boy, and not even Carter's whole body weight would keep the door closed for long.

Then Max was by his side. She grabbed the wooden dead bolt and slid it shut just as Carter's grip began to give way. Max grabbed her brother and dragged him away from the door. It rattled. The handle shook in frustration, and the dead bolt groaned as something pushed against it from the other side. But the lock held, and the door remained closed.

Carter let out a sigh of relief as the handle stopped moving.

Max looked at him and said, "What—"

But she didn't finish, because the door suddenly exploded in a shower of wood as a shape came barreling through it. A man-sized rat stood in the doorway, its powerful shoulders stooped low to fit inside the frame. The creature scanned the room, glancing at Max, but its stare came to rest on Carter. It pulled two wicked-looking knives from a belt strapped across its chest.

Carter met the rat's gaze, and his courage failed him. Numbness born out of terror spread through his body. He couldn't move. He couldn't speak.

Then he heard, from somewhere in the distance, the ringing of bells. Loud and heavy-sounding, like church bells. Carter remembered the bells that had signaled the start of the Piper play in Hamelin. Even as the monster stalked toward him, Carter couldn't help but think of the children scurrying around the stage in their silly rat costumes. This rat was real, and horrible, and it was coming for him.

Voices began calling to each other in the dark, and they were getting closer. The rat cocked his head, momentarily distracted by the new sound, and in that moment Carter's sister acted. Though weaponless, Max still had on her steel-toed boots, and she kicked out at the creature's shin with all the strength her almost-thirteen-year-old body could muster.

It was enough. The rat hissed in pain, dropping one of its knives as it clutched at its wounded leg.

"C'mon!" Max shouted as she hauled Carter to his feet. The rat creature recovered quickly, however, and spun to face them.

"Get behind me!" said Max, and she shoved Carter out of the way as the creature lunged. It was far too big for this tiny room, though, and tripped over one of the beds. As it fell to the floor, it snapped at Carter's and Max's feet. Max jumped back, nearly knocking her brother into the little pig-fat lantern and catching the whole place on fire.

Which gave Carter an idea.

The rat reared up on its knees and snarled at Max, its red eyes flashing in anger. It bared a mouthful of twisted yellow fangs.

Carter grabbed the lantern. *Careful with this,* Lukas had warned.

No need to be careful now, thought Carter, and threw the lantern into the rat's face. The lantern exploded, and hot oil, the pig fat that had been rendered into a thick gel, spilled down one side of the creature's snout, and rivulets of flame snaked across its fur. The rat arched backward and let out a high-pitched squeal of pain and outrage.

Stumbling, it fled through the open doorway and sped off into the night, pawing out the flames as it ran. Then it rounded a darkened street and disappeared.

CHAPTER TWELVE

After the attack, the Watch arrived, and Max and her brother were moved to a new cabin, one with a working door. By the time dawn came, Max's brother had fallen asleep again, only this time with his head in her lap. When she was a little girl, Max used to lay on her mother's lap like that, on nights when she was too stubborn or too scared to sleep in her own bed. They'd sit on the sofa together, watching old black-and-white movies with the living room lights off, and sometimes her father would even join them. The blue light of the TV screen was Max's nightlight, her parents her protectors as she drifted off to sleep.

Tonight, Carter's singular ability to sleep anywhere had paid off for him, while Max, wide awake and afraid, couldn't stop shaking. But in time, the blackness outside turned to blue, then to pink, and a rooster crowed somewhere as it welcomed the sun.

Carter's eyes blinked open. "Was that what I think it was?" he yawned.

"Rooster? Yeah, I guess."

"Cool. My first rooster." Carter kicked off his blankets and rubbed his eyes while Max stretched her legs. The day was already warming up.

"Hey there," said Carter, waving at the boy sitting on the other side of the room. The boy nodded back but didn't say anything. He'd leaned his chair up against the door and had a spear held lazily across his lap.

"Is he the boy you kicked in the . . . ?" whispered Carter.

"I think so," answered Max.

"You have a way of making friends, you know that?"

Max gave her brother a look to shut him up as she tried to work feeling back into her legs. They'd fallen asleep with Carter's big fat head resting on them for the last several hours.

"Are we going to be allowed outside?" Max asked the boy. "Now that it's daytime?"

The boy—Max thought his name was Finn—shrugged. "Lukas said he'd send someone to fetch you. We'll wait."

The Watch had sent one of their own to guard them. Max could have argued—maybe she should have—but the truth was she didn't have any better ideas. The rest of the Watch had spent the remainder of the night searching the village for the rat creature that had attacked them. But the infuriating part had been how this Finn boy had refused to answer her questions. What was that thing doing here, and why had it attacked them? All Finn would say was that Lukas was more suited to answer but that he had better things to do right now. Finn had told Max to wait until morning.

The one piece of information they were able to get out of Finn, and the reason Max had finally stopped pestering him, was that Max and her brother hadn't been the only ones attacked last night. A boy named Pidge had been hurt.

"How's your friend?" Carter asked.

Finn looked up at them. His eyes were bloodshot and tired, and Max suspected she looked much the same.

"I haven't been able to visit him," he answered, with a touch of annoyance in his voice.

Of course. He'd been too busy babysitting them to go check on his friend.

"Do you know what time it is?" Carter asked his sister.

"Early."

"Did you get any sleep?" Carter asked.

"A little," lied Max.

"I can't believe I fell back asleep after . . . you know."

"You needed it."

Carter winced as he tried to rub away a crick in his neck. "Tell you what, though."

"What?"

"You go right on sleeping with your boots on. I strongly support it."

Max allowed herself a little smile for the first time in what seemed like days. Her cheeks felt rusty and out-of-practice.

There was a knock at the door, and Finn motioned for them to stay put while he stepped outside for a moment. Max heard voices, then Finn reappeared, looking relieved. "It's time," he said. "Lukas and Emilie are ready to see you."

They were led back to the village square, past the lone tree Max had seen there yesterday evening. Less than twenty-four hours ago, it had been a tree of naked branches. This morning, however, its boughs were pink with new blossoms. With the dawn, spring had come.

A couple of girls in long skirts and headscarves were keeping an eye on a group of smaller children as they collected fallen blossoms beneath the tree. When the girls spotted Max approaching, one made the sign of the cross over her heart.

What was it with everyone here? They didn't look at Carter that way.

"Wait here," said Finn, and he walked over to a girl sitting in a rocking chair outside a nearby cottage. They whispered together for a few moments, and then the girl opened the front door and gestured for Max and her brother to go inside.

The interior of the cottage smelled good, like baking bread. Someone had set out a light breakfast of sliced apples, fresh bread and smoked meat.

Lukas was seated while standing next to him was a girl Max's age, only taller and broader boned. With her bright blue eyes, paper-fair skin and blond hair barely visible beneath her kerchief, she could have been quite pretty, but her stern expression gave her a hard look, and there were lines around her mouth and forehead—worry lines, Max's mother would have called them. It was odd to see them on the face of a girl so young.

Lukas nodded to Max and her brother but said nothing. He seemed to be waiting for the girl to speak first. Max was suddenly aware that they had not been invited to sit.

"My name is Emilie," said the girl after a few moments of silence. "Lukas tells me that you call yourselves Max and Carter?"

Max made a face. "We call ourselves? Those are our names."

"We'll see about the truth of that," said Emilie, and she walked around the table until she was face to face with Max. "Long ago we learned the telltale signs of wicked magic: the point of the ears, a hidden tail perhaps . . . or hair the *wrong* color."

Max slapped her forehead with her hand. "It's my hair!" she laughed. "That's what everyone's been staring at. My hair is freaking you all out!"

Emilie took a step back, frowning. "So you don't deny it?"

"Well, I'll admit it's pink. But that's only because I dyed it. It's not natural or anything, if that's what you're getting at."

Emilie sniffed. "I know of no pigment that could turn hair that color, nor any sane person who'd want it to."

Max pulled her locks back over her left ear. "Look, you can see where I accidentally dyed my ear, too."

Emilie looked over her shoulder at Lukas, who shrugged and said, "I asked her brother about it, and he, too, says the hair color is false, and that she's always doing things like this. He told me she does it for attention."

Max whirled around on her brother. "I what?"

Carter wouldn't look her in the eye. He just whistled as he stared at the ceiling, but Max made a mental note to make him pay for that later.

Emilie crossed her arms over her chest. "She hurt one of your boys," she said to Lukas, still considering.

"Just his pride," answered Lukas.

"And don't you find it a little too convenient that this girl and her brother show up just hours before a Winter's Moon?" said Emilie. "How many years has it been, Lukas? And now out of nowhere . . ."

"Which is why they are important," said Lukas. "And probably hungry, Emilie."

Emilie didn't drop her skeptical expression, but she did gesture to the table. "Break your fast with us," she said. "And have a seat. There is much to discuss."

Carter plopped onto the bench and began piling up a plate with apples and dried meat. Emilie remained standing, and so Max decided that she would stand, too. She didn't much care for the idea of having to look up at this Emilie girl. She did, however, drink a cup of cool water as her brother struggled to work his teeth through a hunk of smoked pork.

"We need to know the truth about where you came from," said Emilie.

"I already told Lukas everything," said Carter, through a mouthful of food.

"Tell us again," said Emilie.

"We're from New York City," said Max. "We were visiting Hamelin with our father. Not like this New Hamelin village of yours. It's old Hamelin, only like modern . . ." Max found herself distracted by a small rustling sound coming from outside the window, probably just the children playing in the yard, but it was making it hard to keep her facts straight. Max was tired, and this was getting off to a poor start. "Where was I? Look, I don't know what to say. Nothing here makes any sense! What is this place? What was that thing that attacked us?"

"That thing was a rat," answered Emilie stiffly. "And I want to know how it breached our walls and why, out of an entire village of children, he sought *you* out."

"I think we owe them more answers than that, Emilie," said Lukas.

"That's right," said Max. "Because that thing didn't look like any rat I've ever seen. Where did it come from?"

Lukas drew a cloth wrapping from his belt and undid it. Inside was a curved, claw-like knife. The leather handle was well worn, with an oily sheen.

"It came out of the darkness, but that's how it got over the wall," said Lukas. "A knife made for climbing as well as fighting. While most of the Watch was defending the north wall, he used this to scale Pidge's tower. We found the holes driven into the wood there. In last night's confusion, he escaped the same way."

"You mean that thing's still alive?" said Carter.

"Yes, but I'd say you gave him something to remember," said Lukas, winking at Max's brother.

"You still haven't told us what this place is," said Max, her patience gone. As she raised her voice, Max heard that rustle outside the window again—a quick, startled-sounding movement. This time Emilie heard it, too. She held a finger to her lips to ask for quiet as she moved softly across the room. Then, faster than Max would have thought possible, Emilie snatched up a broom and jabbed it through the open window.

There was a chorus of alarmed squawks as a number of black birds took flight.

"Crows?" asked Carter.

"Shoo!" shouted Emilie, still waving the broom out through the window. "Be gone, or I'll call Finn in here with his bow!"

"Wow, what's the problem?" asked Max. "They're just birds."

"No," said Emilie, leveling a look at Max. "They're crows, and that means you have to be careful what you say around them. They're terrible gossips." Then, satisfied that the crows had fled, she set down her broom and straightened her shawl.

Gossiping crows? Well, after giant rat creatures, Max shouldn't have been surprised.

"Now then," Emilie said. "To answer your questions. First of all, this place—"

"Well, it's not earth, I'm pretty sure of that," interrupted Carter as he reached for another strip of smoked pork. Max's brother was a walking stomach. "Last night it was winter, and this morning it's spring. Seasons don't work like that."

"I figured out that much, genius," said Max.

"You both have the right of it, then," said Emilie. "Long ago, we followed a piper wearing a pied cloak into a mountain cave filled with sunlight. He promised us a land of eternal summer, of joy in a place called the Summer Isle, where nothing aged and magic thrived. As you saw last night, that promise was half of a lie."

Max had a flash, just for an instant, of seeing a tunnel of light when the Piper had stolen them away, too.

"From Hamelin were led away one hundred thirty children," her brother recited.

"Yes," said Lukas, taken aback. "How did you know?"

"It's from a story," said Max.

Lukas made a face. "So we've become nothing but a story?"

Max didn't answer. These children didn't seem aware of how long they'd been gone, and maybe time passed differently here, if at all. But in the real world, they'd been missing for over seven hundred years.

"Wait," said Carter. "But if you all came from Hamelin— the real Hamelin back home—then why aren't you speaking German?"

"We are speaking what everyone speaks on the Summer Isle," said Emilie. "There is only one language here. Perhaps it's a part of the magic of this place, but we have always been able to understand the kobolds, even the crows, and they us. Though I must admit the shape of your words are strange."

Max stopped talking, suddenly self-conscious. Now that she paid closer attention, she could see that Lukas's and Emilie's lips didn't quite sync with the words she was hearing in her head.

"Wow, it's like a Babel fish," said Carter, tugging at his ear. "Cool."

"Huh?" said Max.

"From *The Hitchhiker's Guide to the Galaxy*," said her brother. "One of the best books . . . oh, never mind. This place works like a universal translator so that everyone can understand each other no matter what language they're speaking. You need to read more science fiction."

"No, nerd, I don't," said Max. Science fiction, indeed. "So that's how you came here? You followed the Pied Piper?"

Emilie nodded. "We followed his music. The Piper came to Hamelin to rid us of the rats that had plagued our village for years. But when that was done and the Piper demanded his payment, the townsfolk refused. So the Piper returned during the night and cast a spell on the children, too. The music became a dream, and we followed it."

"Something like that happened to us," said Max.

"Only, ours was the exterminator guy," added Carter. "Excuse me, *pest control professional.*"

"If you've heard his song, then you know it's impossible to resist," said Emilie. "I left my village and woke up here, with the rest of the children. Nearly every child from Hamelin who could *walk*." Max caught Emilie and Lukas sharing a look, but before Max had a chance to ask them what it was about, the girl picked up her tale.

"The trees and flowers were so beautiful, but also strange. And the air smelled like honey. At first, we played and danced, and the animals of the forest played with us. The kobolds, the sprites of the forest, taught us songs and games. And we were happy. You have to understand, we'd lived hard lives in our village, filled with backbreaking toil, hungry winters, even seasons of plague. Our new home was so perfect that we didn't give a thought to what we'd left behind. Not at first."

"It actually sounds pretty great," said Max, and she meant it. There was a part of her that dreamed about that very thing.

"It was paradise," agreed Lukas. "It was everything the Piper had promised. The sun never set, not all the way. It never grew darker than twilight, and it never turned cooler than a midsummer's evening. We met kobolds who warned us that there were dangers hidden away in the dark places, witches that lived in the deepest woods, and wicked spirits under the mountains and hills, but we avoided those places. Then one day, everything changed. A morning chill in the air that hadn't been there before became a killing frost by late afternoon. A day that had started out in summer was caught in the dead of winter by evening. And that night, when the sun set, it set for real. True night was upon us for the first time, and a Winter's Moon rose high in the sky."

"We learned, on that first true night, that when the Winter's Moon rises, monsters walk this land," said Emilie.

"The rats," said Max.

"They came out of the dark," said Emilie, nodding. "At first, it was just sounds. Howls, strange gibbering in the night. Shapes that stalked us barely out of sight. But then the rats appeared. We, all of us, grew up terrified of the rats of our village, but as you've seen, these are much worse. They are the monsters of our nightmares."

"They're certainly bigger and smarter than the rats back in Hamelin," said Lukas. "Our scouts tell us the creatures now make their home somewhere in the mountains, though it's said that there were no rats on the Summer Isle before the children of Hamelin arrived. So did we bring them with us? We don't know, but the darkness here has a way of making your fears become real. We can't explain it, but things are . . . born in the dark. Terrible things. It's why we light the village on true nights, why we never sleep in the dark. It's why we walk the walls."

"The Summer Isle may be a dream land when the sun is up," said Emilie. "But when darkness falls, it becomes something else altogether."

Max could hardly believe what she was hearing. She wouldn't have believed if she hadn't seen one of the rat creatures with her own eyes. "How did you all survive?"

"We wouldn't have," said Lukas, "Except the Eldest Boy and the Eldest Girl of our village kept us together. They gave us jobs to do and a purpose. We set about building a fence. That fence grew into a wall, and New Hamelin was born."

"Wow," said Carter, looking at Emilie. "So that means . . ."

Lukas nodded. "Emilie is the Eldest Girl. We would've been lost on that first night if not for her." Emilie made a *tsk*ing sound and waved the compliment away, but she didn't deny it.

"And that makes you Eldest Boy," said Max.

"I am now," said Lukas, looking down. "But I wasn't then. That was Marc. And Leon after him. I just did what I was told."

"And where are they now?" asked Carter. "Did they retire or something?"

Max winced. She could guess what had happened.

"They were lost," said Lukas quietly. "I'm just the next in line."

Carter quietly chewed on his breakfast as he absorbed what Lukas was saying. Children had been *lost*.

"We've learned much since then," said Lukas. "Kobold rumors mostly, and kobolds lie a lot. But they tell of a time before, when the Summer Isle wasn't the wild and dangerous land that it is today. They say it was once a magical kingdom, but things began to change when two powerful magicians sailed to shore. The magicians are known as the Piper and the Peddler."

"Wait," said Max. "Did you just say the *Peddler*?"

"Yes," said Lukas. "He doesn't go by any other name. Why, have you heard of him?"

The story of the Piper and the Peddler was the lost fairy tale their father had been after, the one listed in the earliest version of the Grimm collection. Surely it wasn't just coincidence, but Max didn't know how to explain it to these children, much less what it meant. Most of all, Max hadn't decided yet if she could trust them.

"No," said Max. "I . . . I just thought you said something else. Forget it. Keep going."

Carter gave Max a look. Her little brother had always been too good at sniffing out lies, even little ones. Thankfully he didn't say anything.

"The Peddler travels the land still," said Lukas. "You might have seen his road outside the village. That magic road is what keeps at least some of the wildness at bay. They say that the magicians were two of the most powerful beings on the Summer Isle, along with the Princess of the Elves, but we've never even seen her. She never leaves her castle on the other side of the isle."

At the mention of the Princess, Emilie scowled, but she didn't interrupt.

"Something happened between the two magicians," continued Lukas. "Some kind of battle, and it happened right after we arrived."

"So you think they fought because of what the Piper did to you all?" asked Max. "Because he kidnapped you?"

"The Peddler sometimes visits New Hamelin, and I've asked him that myself," said Lukas. "But he's an old man, and he refuses to answer most of my questions—he pretends he can't hear me. All that I've been able to get out of him is that the magicians did fight, and the Piper lost. I think the Princess of the Elves helped the Peddler, but I'm not sure. After the battle, the Piper was locked away in a secret prison, and the Princess retreated to her castle. Evil spread. The Winter Moons came more often. The rats appeared and began plaguing the isle."

"The rats don't grow crops, and they don't keep live-stock," said Emilie. "They take what they need from others and spoil the rest."

Rat creatures. Kobolds and elves. A magician who stole children away to a twisted, magic fairyland where children never grew up but nightmares became reality. Max remembered what Mrs. Amsel had said about the original villagers of Hamelin, about the things in the forest they'd feared—*the dark magic of the world,* she'd called it. It looked like they'd been right after all.

Of course, none of this answered the questions foremost on Max's mind. "If the Piper is locked up, then how did he bring us here?" asked Max. "And why? And how do we get home again?"

"I was hoping you could tell *us*," said Lukas. "We haven't seen the Piper since the night he stole us away. No one has."

"And you haven't tried to find another way home?"

Lukas stared at her, a slow smile creeping across his face. Max exchanged a worried glance with Carter. Lukas was starting to freak them both out.

"Thanks to you," Lukas said, "I think we just have."

"That's enough," said Emilie, cutting Lukas off. "They are two children, that is all. Two more children in a village full of children."

"You don't know that, Emilie," said Lukas.

"We won't talk about it now," said Emilie. "They've had enough for one day, surely."

"Wait," said Max. "Whatever it is, I want to talk about it! You can't just order us around."

Lukas looked like he wanted to say more, but Emilie rapped her knuckles against the table. "We will speak no more of it today!" she said, glaring at Max. "There are too many interested in you already." With this, Emilie shot a glance at the window where she'd scared off the crows, then to Lukas, who reluctantly nodded.

"Tomorrow," he said.

"In the meantime, Max and Carter are welcome in New Hamelin," Emilie continued. "You will be given a cottage of your own, food to eat and chores to do. To survive, we work hard, but survive we do. I hope that you can come to think of this place as home."

Emilie adjusted her shawl and looked directly at Max. "But remember that your ways are not our ways. You must follow our rules, even if they seem strange to you. And know," she added with a warning look, "that I am always watching you."

With that warning, Emilie finally sat down in her chair and cried out in shock as a long, sputtering sound, much like a fart, escaped from beneath her seat cushion.

❧ CHAPTER THIRTEEN ❧

Emilie asked Lukas to show Max and Carter to the cottage that would be their new home. They were to be given Leon's house, which was small for two people but safely situated near the center of the village and nicely upwind of the pigpens. The cottage had remained empty in memory of New Hamelin's former captain, but it was time that it be put to use again—space couldn't be wasted in the little walled village. But first, Lukas wanted to show Max and Carter something else. Something secret.

"There, I think that's far enough," he said once they'd gotten out of sight of the village square.

"Far enough for what?" asked Max.

"Far enough that Emilie won't see what I'm about to do," answered Lukas. "Come on." Then he turned and began leading them in the opposite direction, through the twisting streets of New Hamelin, and he didn't stop until they'd reached the front gate. Children stopped and stared as he led Max and Carter through the village, but Lukas didn't slow down. While the Elder Girl had no real authority to tell the Elder Boy what to do, Lukas had yet to find the courage to stand up to Emilie. That was about to change.

When Lukas ordered the guards to open the front gate, it earned him even more stares, but they obeyed. Two boys put their shoulders against the massive log that served as the gate's giant dead bolt. It had been greased with pig fat so that it could be easily slid in and out of place, and once it was unbolted, a third guard cranked the winch that swung the gate open wide. Outside, an expansive field of grass and flowers stretched onward, butting up against the border of the Shimmering Forest. The Peddler's Road disappeared into those trees, continuing its long journey across the isle. Lukas strode past Max and Carter, who were looking concerned, and planted himself outside the gate. A warm summer breeze stirred the grass in the fields, causing it to ripple like waves. It was a welcome change from the biting winter winds of the night before.

"I remember when I was little," began Lukas, "a man, who must have been my father, used to tell me stories about the woods outside our old village. *Don't stray from the path,* he'd say, *or else the elves will steal you away. And don't leave the milk uncovered or the kobolds will bathe in it and cause it to spoil.* He told me the church bell rang at dawn to frighten away the night's wicked spirits and the iron horseshoes we hung above our door would keep the goblins out. My father's stories."

Lukas drew his sword and considered it. Such an ugly thing, and not something he'd ever wanted. Although Marc had first wielded it, Leon had held it the longest, and Leon had been Lukas's friend. The sword of the Eldest Boy would always be Leon's, no matter what anyone else said. Lukas drove the sword's point into the soft earth.

"Those stories were full of monsters, and they were frightening, but fascinating, too, you understand? Full of magic. On the rare occasions that he did allow me to go with him into the woods, to pick mushrooms or collect kindling, my heart would beat so fast I thought that every elf and ogre within miles had to be able to hear it. But I never saw one. Not one. The stories weren't real, you see, until I came here."

"Lukas," said Max, still inside the gate with Carter, "what are we doing here?" She looked at him suspiciously, as if she expected him to pull her and her brother outside, then run back in and close the gate behind them. Lukas tried to reassure her with a smile.

"I want to explain," he said, coming back inside the open gate. "Because in this place, elves are real. Ogres wander the woods, and kobolds are mischievous and bothersome at the best of times. Just like the stories said. We mostly stay inside our walls, except for the scouts. We try to avoid other folk here on the Summer Isle. It's too easy to get lost out there in all the magic."

Lukas plucked his sword back out of the dirt and held it up to the sun, pointing at the road. The blade was a dull black that refused to reflect the light at all. Such an ugly thing.

"The Peddler's Road crosses from one edge of the isle to

the other, and the Peddler walks it, trading with anyone he meets."

"He's one of the magicians you and Emilie were talking about," said Carter.

Lukas nodded. "On his first visit to our village, many, many years ago, he gave Marc this sword. Traded it for a song, or so the story goes."

"What does this Peddler guy have to do with us?" said Max, peering out at the road and the distant woods. "Do you plan on trading us in for two more-useful lost children?"

Lukas laughed. Emilie had already taken a dislike to Max's humor, but Lukas appreciated it. She wasn't like the other girls in New Hamelin. She wasn't like anyone he'd ever met. Neither was her brother, for that matter, which was why Lukas knew they were special.

"Everyone in New Hamelin has traded with the Peddler at one time or another," said Lukas. "Some have been happier with their trades than others." Lukas removed a leather scroll case from his belt and opened it up. "This is what he gave to me."

"Cool," said Carter. "A map."

It was a map indeed. A map that Lukas had memorized years ago. It wasn't impressive to look at, just a rough drawing of the Summer Isle, and not even drawn to scale. Finn said that the island reminded him of a butterfly, but Lukas had always thought it looked more like a flower. New Hamelin was clearly labeled between the northern mountains and the Shimmering Forest. The Great River nearly cut the land in two before splitting into the smaller Western

Fork and Eastern Fork, and then those continued on until they emptied into the sea. How many countless hours had Lukas spent staring at this map until he knew every ink stroke by heart?

Winding through the isle was a thin dotted line.

"Is that . . . ," asked Max.

"Yes, that is the Peddler's Road. I was told this map was drawn by human hands, or close enough, and I believe it. The rats certainly didn't make it, and the kobolds have no use for such things. Books, maps and writing of any kind are all pointless in their eyes. They don't even like art, unless it's a picture of one of them."

Carter held out his hands, and Lukas laid the map gently across them so the boy could get a better look. Max peered over her brother's shoulder, and Lukas watched their faces as they studied it. Would he see something in their expressions? A special recognition or understanding of what it really meant? Or would that be too easy?

"The Peddler promised me that this map was special," said Lukas. "Because it once belonged to a witch who could see the future. The Peddler told me that it was difficult to come by, but that it was worth it because this map came with a prophecy: *Only when the last son of Hamelin appears and the Black Tower found will the Piper's prison open and the children return safe and sound.*"

"What's that supposed to mean?" asked Carter.

Lukas looked at Carter. The boy really did remind Lukas of Timm, and it wasn't because of his leg. It was because Timm had been a brave boy, too, though he would never have admitted it. It was funny how Lukas could remember his old friend so clearly, yet he couldn't even picture his own parents' faces.

"I think it means that the last son of Hamelin will lead us home," said Lukas after a moment. "And here you are."

"But Carter's *not* a son of Hamelin," said Max. "We're from New York City."

"But you came to us from Hamelin," said Lukas. "The Piper led you two here for a reason."

"Well," said Carter. "*Led* might be the wrong word. Kidnapped, maybe."

"There's something else," said Lukas, and he pointed to the northeastern corner of the map, at the hills on the other side of the Great River. Nestled in those hills was a black tower. Even now, just seeing it made Lukas's heart race.

"Oh, come on," said Max, squinting down at the tiny drawing. "Look, if the Peddler's going to mention a black tower in his so-called prophecy, then of course he'd draw a little black tower on the map he's trying to sell you."

"No," said Lukas. His excitement was rising, and his hands were shaking. He felt like he was going to trip over his words if he didn't get them out fast enough. "You don't understand, that tower wasn't there yesterday morning!"

"What do you mean?" asked Max.

"I've had this map for ages," said Lukas. "I look at it every day, and there was no tower on this map until the day you two appeared."

"Whoa," said Carter.

"The tower has been found," said Lukas. "All we need to do is follow the Peddler's Road and it'll take us there! See?"

Lukas traced the little dotted line through the forests,

across the river and clear to the other side of the isle. The road went all the way to the eastern coast.

"But it doesn't go all the way," said Carter, pointing at it. "We'd have to leave the road at this Deep Forest here and head north."

"Across the Dark Moors, yes," said Lukas. That part of the journey was worrisome, but it was no use dwelling on it now. Not yet, and not in front of Max and her brother. "But it would be easy travel until then."

"Wait," said Max. "Why didn't Emilie mention any of this?"

Lukas sighed. "Because she's spent a long time building us a home that we can be safe in. She doesn't like the idea of anyone leaving it. Not without a very good reason."

"And this isn't a good reason?" asked Carter. "What's Emilie's problem, anyway?"

Lukas shrugged. It was easy to dislike Emilie, partly because the girl worked hard to keep others at a distance. But what Carter and his sister didn't understand, what they might never understand, was that for all these years Emilie had been the one person who'd kept the village together, who'd held them when they had nightmares and told them stories when they couldn't sleep. She'd been more than just the Eldest Girl—she'd been New Hamelin's mother. It was hard for her to let go.

"But do you trust this Peddler person?" asked Max. "How do you know you can believe him?"

"Two days ago, I wasn't sure I did believe," said Lukas. "What if everything the Peddler told me was just a story?

But then you two showed up, and I was reminded of something I had almost forgotten."

"What?" asked Carter.

"Here on the Summer Isle, *stories are real!*" Lukas smiled broadly and clapped Max and Carter on their shoulders. "So, what do you say? Are you up for an adventure?"

CHAPTER FOURTEEN

"It's not fair that you get to decide," said Carter. "You won't even talk about it!"

"There's nothing to talk about," said Max. "That rat creature came from *out there,* and so we not going *out there* where there are more of them. Discussion over."

Max turned her back on her brother and busied herself with making up their beds, such as they were. The beds here in New Hamelin were thin, stitched mattresses stuffed with some kind of moss that felt like cotton, and the blankets were woven of coarse wool. And though Lukas had promised that they were upwind of the pigs, there was still a distinct smell of manure at this end of the village. Still, the cottage was comfortable enough, if spare. With nothing else to do but argue with her brother, Max had made and re-made her own bed at least four times over the last half hour.

Carter was upset, but he would get over it. Actually, Max

found she didn't much care if he did get over it, as there was no way they were going with Lukas on this silly quest, no matter how Carter felt about it. She wouldn't drag her little brother through monster-infested woods just because of a tiny black tower on a map.

"Then how do we get home?" asked Carter, plopping himself onto the bed Max had just made. "If we can't go with Lukas, then how do we get home?"

"I don't know yet," admitted Max. "But running off right now isn't the answer. Carter, we don't even know what's out there! Every time I turn around I keep hoping we'll wake up and be back home. I still don't know what's going on."

"It's like Lukas and Emilie said—we're in a magic land," said Carter. "Didn't you ever wonder where the Pied Piper of Hamelin took all those children? Well, now we know."

Max stared at her brother. "And you believe all that? This place doesn't make any sense. Rat creatures and a village full of children who never grew up . . ."

"Max," said Carter. "It's a *magic land.*"

"There's no such thing as magic!" said Max.

"Why do you have such a hard time believing in this?" said Carter. "Look around you! It's just like one of Dad's stories."

"Exactly! And that's all they are—stories. I don't care what Lukas says. Stories aren't real. Not here, not anywhere."

"But the map—"

"I don't want to hear any more about it!" snapped Max. "You're not Mom."

"Nope," said Max, taking a deep breath. "And, believe me, this is turning out to be the worst babysitting job in the *history* of babysitting jobs, but I'm older, and that puts me in charge. Deal with it."

Carter fell back onto the bed and stared at the ceiling. From the sound of his breathing—quick, in and out through his nose—Max could tell that he was still angry with her, probably more so now that she'd played the older-sister card on him. If he wanted to punish her with the silent treatment, he could go right ahead, but there weren't any parents around to tell her she had to stay in the same room with him.

"I'm going for a walk," said Max, to which Carter said nothing. When she walked out, the door gave a satisfying slam. She'd made a good exit, at least.

Max wandered through the streets and marveled yet again at the strangeness that was the village of New Hamelin. If she were to accept all of this at face value, like Carter had, then these children had been born in the thirteenth century. It was too incredible, that they were the sons and daughters of carpenters and blacksmiths, farmers, woodsmen and probably even a few soldiers. Still, despite the quirks in some of the architecture, and the way the streets twisted and turned without any real purpose, these children had accomplished an amazing feat in building this village. Children from back home would have been lost. Max herself kept reflexively reaching for her phone that wasn't there.

Max spotted a rope bridge strung between two cottages on opposite sides of the street. A few younger boys— *middles,* Lukas would have called them—were dangling their bare feet over the bridge and watching the passersby below. Every now and then, someone would try to leap up and grab their feet, but the boys always managed to pull away just in time. It was an odd game, like seeing who could jump up and touch the light fixture in the ceiling, but Max supposed it passed the hours. Now and then someone would get close enough to succeed in tapping the bottoms of the boys' feet, and the boys would clap and holler. If someone missed completely, there were boos and hisses from above.

When the boys saw Max coming, however, they quickly pulled their feet out of range. Like most everyone else she passed, they stopped and stared. By now Max should've been used to it, but the constant double takes and the little gasps whenever she rounded a corner had started to become very annoying. She should've dyed her hair bright green. That would've really given these kids something to whisper about.

Max left the boys to their play and eventually wandered by the source of the terrible manure smell. It was a pigpen, where several girls were wrestling a hog the size of a donkey back into its corner. It was ridiculous work to be trying to accomplish in long skirts, but the girls seemed determined to do it. Emilie had mentioned assigning chores to Max and her brother, and Max didn't know how long the two of them would be trapped here, but chasing pigs through the mud would have to be a deal breaker.

As she wound her way back toward the village square, she found another group of girls tending a small house garden. Despite the hot sun overhead (and what a change that was from yesterday), these girls were also wearing long skirts and long-sleeved shirts as they dug up carrots from the little patch of land. The kerchiefs around their heads were already soaked with sweat.

Girls chasing pigs. Girls harvesting crops. While boys sat around wiggling their toes at people. A look up at the gate wall confirmed something that Max had already suspected—there weren't any skirts up there. Nor were there any climbing up and down the bell towers or patrolling the streets. The boys were charged with defending New Hamelin while the girls were made to slop the pigs and harvest crops.

After that, it took exactly two seconds for Max to decide what chore she wanted to be assigned to.

Emilie's cottage looked out onto the Summer Tree in the village square. She was sitting in a rocking chair on her porch as she snapped beans and dropped them into a tall bucket. Small children seemed to always be playing under the Summer Tree, and Max guessed that it served as a kind of day care for the younger ones, under Emilie's watchful eye. It made sense, since it was probably the safest place in the entire village.

Emilie gave Max a curt nod when she spotted her, but she didn't say hello. Max strode right up to her porch. "I've decided what chore I want," said Max.

"Oh?" said Emilie. "I thought you might be coming to tell me that you and your brother were leaving with Lukas." Emilie snapped another bean in two, as if for emphasis.

Surprised, Max cocked her head at the girl. "How did you know about that?"

"I know more about what goes on in this village than Lukas gives me credit for," said Emilie. "So are you?"

"What? Going in search of some black tower that may or

may not even exist? I'm not dragging my brother out there without a better reason than an ink spot on a map."

Emilie paused. "That's good. You have more sense than I'd guessed."

"Uh, thanks?" said Max. That was probably the closest thing to a compliment she was going to get from this sour-faced girl. Ever.

"Tea?" asked Emilie. She gestured to a small table, where a kettle and two wooden mugs were set upon a tray.

"Sure," said Max. She supposed it would be pointless to ask if there was any coffee around. "Were you expecting company?"

"I get many visitors throughout the day," said Emilie. "From solving arguments over borrowed tools to treating children with fevers, my role as Eldest Girl comes with many responsibilities."

"Yeah, I guess so."

Emilie began to pour the tea. "You said you'd decided on a chore? You see something you might be good at?"

"Yes," said Max. "I want to join the Watch."

Emilie froze. She'd finished pouring one cup of tea but the second still stood empty. Then she straightened up and looked at Max. "I'm afraid the Watch is the most important role in all of New Hamelin. Our lives depend on them doing their job. It's not for girls."

On the one hand, Max could hardly believe she was hearing this; on the other, it was exactly what she'd expected. "But how can you say that? I mean, you're a girl."

"Yes," said Emilie. "And I know the proper roles for our

sex. We mend and we tend. The only watching we do is after the little ones out there under the tree."

"That is so . . . medieval!"

"I don't even know what that word means, but girls are not warriors," said Emilie, and she quite pointedly set down the kettle, leaving the second cup still empty. It looked like her offer had been rescinded. "Since coming here, many of us have been forced to do things we never thought we'd have to, but we hold to what traditions we can. I told you, our ways are not your ways."

"Right," said Max. "That's why *you* won't be joining the Watch. *I* will."

"Girls in this village do not fight!" said Emilie, and her cheeks began to color with anger.

"No, but they do lead," said Max.

"What's that supposed to mean?"

"How many female mayors, or whatever you people called them, did you have back in old Hamelin?"

"I'm not—"

"You're the Eldest Girl," said Max. "I see how people treat you. Lukas might be called Eldest Boy, but it's obvious who wears the pants around here." At that Emilie let out a startled little gasp. "Sorry," said Max. "I didn't mean pants literally. It's just an expression. Although you all could use a few pairs."

"I think you'd better—"

"Look, I don't know how much of all *this* I believe." Max gestured to the village around them, "But it looks like you got the job of leading these people because you earned it. Lukas said so—you kept them all together. Heck, you kept them *alive*. You proved that leading has nothing to do with being a boy or a girl, so why should only boys be asked to risk their lives up on that wall, or out scouting those woods? Why shouldn't girls be allowed to, if they choose? And let a few boys chase the pigs while you're at it."

Emilie took a long drink of her tea. She seemed to be studying Max, judging her, maybe. Hopefully, she was thinking over what Max had said, but just when Max thought that the girl's stony exterior might crack, Emilie set the cup down and cleared her throat. "I suggest you consider working in the bread kitchen. Or we could always use help with the little ones. Your brother's leg will keep him off the wall and out of the bell towers, but lamplighting is a respectable job. You may let me know your preference in the morning, otherwise I will assign you one."

Emilie stood up and adjusted her shawl. "Tonight there will be a feast in the square, a *tradition* we have here in New Hamelin. Lukas asked specifically for you to attend, and I would be honored if you and your brother would sit at my table. Good day, Max."

Then Emilie turned and went inside. Her door, it turned out, slammed just as well as Max's had.

⊰ CHAPTER FIFTEEN ⊱

By the time Carter and his sister had gotten their food and made their way back to Emilie's table, the sun had already started to dip low beneath the trees.

"Don't worry," said Emilie, noticing Carter's anxious glances up at the sky. "The sun won't go down tonight. We've never had two true nights in a row, and the rats are cowardly without the darkness to hide them. We won't have anything to worry about this evening."

Carter nodded, relieved. The air was as warm as midsummer, unlike last night's brutal cold. Come morning, the sun would reverse course in the sky and start another day. Whatever this place was, the laws of celestial bodies didn't apply here.

The entire village, with the exception of the Watch on duty at the gate wall, had gathered in the square. Some were seated on benches, others on the grass beneath the Summer

Tree, and everyone was sharing in the largest potluck dinner Carter had ever seen. It needed to be; there had to be enough to feed over a hundred hungry children. Plates were piled high with grilled vegetables—some recognizable or at least similar to those back home. There were peas and carrots, but there were other things, such as some kind of purplish root almost exactly the length of his forearm. A variety of brightly colored berries were served in sweet syrup. Skewers of meat, mostly pork, roasted over an open fire pit. The smells of good things cooking, blended with the already sweet air of the Summer Isle, made Carter dizzy with hunger.

He'd felt guilty at first that they had nothing to contribute to the feast, but he soon set about drowning that guilt in gluttony. A few older boys laughed when they saw the mountain of food Carter had balanced on his plate, but it seemed a good-natured laugh, and one of them even gave him a friendly pat on the shoulder as he passed by.

His sister, of course, barely nibbled. Max seemed determined not to enjoy herself, not even a tiny bit. Carter suspected that she'd gone out of her way to pick only the most unappetizing foods as a way to add to her misery. A few slimy-looking mushrooms and a hunk of stale bread was all she took. The Crouch was heavy on her shoulders again, and since Max couldn't shake her sour mood, she'd wallow in it.

Carter should've been the one pouting; after all wasn't Max getting her way? They weren't going to try to find a way home. He knew that Max was scared, no matter how his sister tried to hide it—how could she not be? They'd been attacked last night by a real-life monster. Even Carter had been sure that they were both going to die. But they hadn't. They had fought the monster . . . and won.

And everyone in the village knew about it. Max seemed to think that all the staring was because they were different, and while that might have been true at first, Carter could see a change had come over the children of New Hamelin. He saw it in their faces, he heard it in their whispers at dinner. Carter and Max were heroes.

That's what Max was missing, and it was a brand-new feeling for Carter. He'd spent most of his life trying to avoid being noticed. Stay inconspicuous, don't make too much noise and don't draw attention to yourself. That was how you survived when you were smaller and brighter than the rest, and when you had to walk while the other kids ran. But the children of New Hamelin were looking at him in a different way. This time he didn't feel like hiding, and he didn't mind the staring. This time the staring felt good.

Now Max was trying her very best to ruin it. Carter wasn't sure if he wanted to help the children of New Hamelin because they needed it, or if he only wanted to go on playing the hero, but either way, Lukas's plan was a better idea than hiding here in the village and waiting for the next Winter's Moon—the next attack. Maybe the prophecy of his was telling the truth. What if the Black Tower was real, and what if the way home lay inside it? Carter could make this journey, though he knew it wouldn't be easy, and if *he* could, then so could Max. If that meant slaying the invisible Crouch on her shoulders or dragging her along by her pink hair, then Carter would have to do it. Because this was their heroes' journey. They had to go.

Emilie had seated them at her table for dinner. It was obviously a place of honor, which meant that no one at the table actually talked to each other. He shouldn't have been surprised. Between Emilie, Carter and Max, nearly everyone there was mad at someone for something.

Carter had just begun to think about getting seconds when Emilie stood and began calling for quiet. Carter feared a speech was coming, and he dearly wished he'd have thought far enough ahead to get dessert. In a land where the air smelled this sweet, there were bound to be some spectacular treats.

The crowd took only a few moments to settle. It was impressive how quickly Emilie could quiet an entire village of children. "I remember . . . ," she began, in a voice loud enough for all to hear.

I knew it, thought Carter, shaking his head in disappointment. *A speech.*

"I remember last night's Winter's Moon," said Emilie, "and I remember the first night long ago, and I honor those who we have lost to the darkness over the years. I honor Pidge, who is not yet lost to us and who is in our thoughts now."

Emilie bowed her head as the rest of the village followed suit. Carter put his own head down but peeked up at Max as he did so. Her head wasn't bowed; she just sat back in her chair, her face expressionless. Max never stood during the Pledge of Allegiance, either. It was embarrassing.

After a moment of silence, Emilie continued. "But I also remember the Time Before. I remember kneading dough next to my mother. I remember the feel of it sticking beneath my fingernails and her gently chiding me to wash them better and to keep my nails trim. I remember that."

Emilie sat back down and was quiet as she stared into her cup. No one was saying anything, and Carter found himself wishing someone would cough, just to break the silence. But then another girl stood up, one of the older girls, and said, "I remember my brother. I think he was my brother, though he was almost a man. I remember him tousling my hair whenever he left the house to go with father to work. His hands were rough and callused, but he was gentle. I remember that."

On and on the recitation went, as different New Hameliners stood and shared memories of their lives before coming to the Summer Isle. It might be a memory of their parents or even a favorite pet. Most seemed inconsequential on the surface—memories of chores or some dull daily task—but the children's voices were filled with emotion as they spoke.

Then another boy stood. He was one of the middles and not that much younger than Carter. "I . . . ," the boy began. "I can't. I can't remember anything. It's all gone. They're all gone."

Then Emilie was at his side, her arms around him. The boy was crying softly into her shoulder. Looking around, there were many faces like his, some nodding sadly, others holding on to each other for comfort. "We will remember for you," Emilie was saying. "For as long as we can."

Others stood and confessed the same, that the memories of their families and of the Time Before had faded into mist. Carter thought of his own father, back at home, and for the first time since their arrival in New Hamelin, he felt a stab of homesickness. What must their father think? How worried he must be. What had happened to him? Carter felt guilty that it had taken him this long to worry.

"Max," said Carter, but when he turned around, she was gone, her seat empty. He spotted her in the distance, walking away from the gathering.

Carter almost chased after her, but he stopped himself. She wanted to be alone. Maybe she was thinking the same things he was. Maybe she'd been reminded that they had a father, a mother and a life waiting for them back home, and that if they stayed here in New Hamelin, they might never see them again.

As Carter turned back around in his seat, he noticed that he wasn't the only one watching his sister go. Emilie's face was unreadable, but she was watching, too.

CHAPTER SIXTEEN

Max found Lukas standing atop the gate wall. He'd positioned himself where he could keep an eye on the village and on the wilderness beyond. Though the sky was only a purple twilight, the shadows up here were thick in places, and Max nearly stumbled and fell as she stepped along the narrow walkway.

"Careful," said Lukas. "It's a long way down."

"Right," said Max. She glanced behind her at the nearly thirty-foot drop to the hard ground below. "Thanks for the warning. A little late, though."

"You left early," said Lukas, gesturing back toward the feast. "The remembrances can't be half over."

"You are a total jerk wad," said Max. "And you're horrible. You and Emilie."

Lukas didn't look surprised. "I'm not sure I know the expression, but I guess a *jerk wad* is nothing good."

"You knew what we would hear tonight," said Max. "You knew what Emilie was going to do, and that's why you wanted us there."

"The First Night Supper is a tradition as old as this village," said Lukas. "The remembrances are a part of that."

"But there was a boy who couldn't even remember his own family!" said Max, her voice cracking as her eyes blurred with tears. She absolutely hated when she cried out of anger.

"No, he can't remember them," answered Lukas, matter-of-factly. "Most of the middles can't. The elders have only a few memories of the Time Before. I can tell you I had a mother, and a father, but I can't tell you what they looked like. I dream of them sometimes, but I don't know how much of the dream is memory and how much is just wishing."

Lukas put an arm on Max's shoulder, and thinking he was trying to comfort her, she instinctively tried to shove it away. But his grip remained firm, and instead of pulling her close, he turned her around so that she was facing away from the village and out into the wild beyond. "We've held on for as long as we can, Max," he said. "But if the rats don't get us, this place will. It makes you forget who you really are."

In the dim twilight Max could see the distant tree-tops and the winding road beneath an orange and purple horizon that seemed to go on forever. Floating lights, like large fireflies, shimmered beneath the trees. The Summer Isle looked so peaceful, so beautiful, but then a scream tore through the air as some creature met its end out there in the wilderness, and the cry was followed by a second, rougher howl that echoed with triumph. It made the hairs on the back of her neck stand on end. The Summer Isle was a wild place, untamed and magical.

"What's it like up here on the gate wall?" asked Max. "On a true night?"

Lukas sighed. "It's scary. You see things out there in the dark. Sometimes it's the rats, sometimes it's other things— things I don't even have names for. They just appear out of nowhere, I can't really explain it. If you're lucky, they will go away after a while, they'll retreat into the blackness."

"And if you're unlucky?"

"If you're unlucky, they try to climb the wall."

Max hugged herself to keep from shivering. "The world back home's not the same place you left, Lukas. Not even close. It's been, like, hundreds of years."

Lukas chewed on his lip for a moment as he absorbed this. Max had expected the news to be a shock, but the boy just shook his head. "Some of us suspected as much, but time doesn't pass the same here. The years are hazy, and they go by in a fog. The prophecy says your brother will lead us *home,* Max, but I'm not even sure what that word means anymore. Maybe we can go back to where and *when* we came from. Or maybe not. Maybe everything we know is truly dead and gone. But if we stay here, at best we'll forget who we are. At worst . . ."

Lukas didn't finish what he was about to say, but he didn't need to. Max sniffed and wiped her nose with the back of her arm. She left a streak of snot from her elbow to her wrist. "Wow, that's gross," she said.

"Yes, it is," Lukas agreed, with a slight grin.

"What did the prophecy say again? What did it say exactly?"

"Only when the last son of Hamelin appears and the Black Tower found will the Piper's prison open and the children return safe and sound. If there was more than that, the Peddler never told it to me."

"One sentence," said Max. "You're asking us to risk a lot for one sentence. You're asking us to risk everything."

Lukas nodded. "I know. But the Black Tower has appeared, I know it, and we have the map of where to find it. I don't see any better ideas."

"Swear to me you won't let Carter get hurt. Swear it, Lukas."

Lukas's face turned suddenly grim. "I swear it, Max. I'll die first."

"You're really dramatic, you know that?" Max sighed. "You really think this prophecy is for real? You think this tower of yours can help us find the way home?"

"I do. And I think your brother is up to the task. More so than you know."

Max took a deep breath. Her throat was sore from crying. "Okay. We'll go with you, but you'd better be right."

"I am. And thank you."

"One other thing."

"Yes?" he said.

Max looked back out over the dark, alien landscape. The evening had grown quiet again. Whatever thing had howled moments ago was probably busy with its fresh meal, but what else was out there? In a magical land where anything could happen, everything could be dangerous.

Max looked Lukas in the eye. "I want a spear."

⇥ CHAPTER SEVENTEEN ⇤

I f Lukas had hoped their small party would be able to sneak away without attracting attention, he should have thought about that before inviting Paul along. The plan had been to leave at dawn, but there was a crowd of onlookers assembled at the front gate before Lukas had even arrived. Paul must've spent the entire evening bragging about their upcoming adventure. The gate was now crowded with middles, elders, a few of the youngest ones holding the hands of the older girls, and all were watching him with looks of expectation. And fear. No one wanted to be without their captain.

He wondered what stories Paul's rumor mongering had given birth to. There hadn't been time to tell Paul the whole truth behind their expedition, and Lukas knew that any holes in Paul's version would be filled in with wild speculations, but it couldn't be helped. The fewer who knew about the prophecy the better. Lukas didn't want to break their hearts if he failed.

Paul himself was uncharacteristically on time, flanked by Finn and another scout. Paul carried his pack on one shoulder and a quiver of arrows slung over the other. The boy leaned on his unstrung bow and yawned. "Must all adventures start at dawn?" he complained. "Has anyone ever tried setting out at noon?"

Finn let out an exasperated sigh. The scout leader had taken it upon himself to get Paul here promptly, and Finn's wake-up calls were anything but gentle.

"I want to cover as much ground as possible before evening," said Lukas. "And, by the way," he added in a whisper, "what are all these people doing here at the start of our *secret* mission?"

Paul shrugged, and glanced at the crowd, unconcerned. "I don't know. Admiring the dawn?"

Lukas scowled as he hefted up his own heavy pack and did a quick inventory of their gear. He'd wanted to travel light, but he'd had to pack for Max and her brother as well. They wouldn't have known what to bring out into the wild.

"I've sent Tomas to fetch the newcomers," said Finn. "And to deliver the . . . *items* you requested." The scout's mouth turned at the word. Lukas knew what Finn must think of giving weapons away, especially to a girl, but a deal was a deal.

"Thank you," said Lukas. "And, since you will be Eldest Boy in my absence, I want you to have this."

He unbuckled the sword from around his waist, but Finn reached out his hand to stop him. "That belongs to you," said Finn.

"It's the Sword of the Eldest Boy," said Lukas. "While I'm gone, that's you."

"You're traveling the Peddler's Road, not storming the rat king's tunnels, for goodness' sake!" said Finn.

But Lukas and Finn both knew that traveling the Peddler's Road was no simple journey. The only creature on the Summer Isle entirely safe on the road was the Peddler himself. No one knew what dangers might be encountered along the way, though Lukas didn't think it wise to say that out loud. Not with so many ears listening.

"This isn't a request," said Lukas. "It's an order. My last one until I get back."

Reluctantly, Finn took the sword. He made a sour face as he tested the weight. Lukas knew the feeling. "I'm even worse with a sword than you are, you know," said Finn. "Just as likely cut my own head off as any rat's."

"Then you'd better practice," said Lukas. One of the other boys of the Watch handed Lukas a long-handled hatchet with an iron-banded blade. A hatchet was better for a long journey, anyhow. Hopefully, he'd only need it to cut firewood.

He'd just finished sliding the hatchet into his belt when Paul gave a quick warning cough. All eyes had turned to watch a small group making its way through the crowd. Max and Carter were walking side by side, the boy's face looking bright and cheerful, in contrast to his sister's, which was as sunny as a rain cloud. People were whispering because of the armored vest of thick leather Max wore and the spear balanced against her shoulder. The armor and the weapon were marks of the Watch; they belonged to the Watch, and no girl in the history of New Hamelin had ever been allowed to carry them before. But again, a deal was a deal.

Carter had been given a hooded traveling cloak treated with oil to keep the rain off and his own small backpack. He carried a stout walking stick to lean on and wore a little knife tucked into his belt. The boy had wanted a spear as well, but both Lukas and Max had refused to let him have one. The whole point was to keep Carter away from any fighting, and not just because of Lukas's promise—Carter was the last son of New Hamelin, and if the prophecy was to be believed, then the future of the whole village might hinge on his safety.

But it wasn't the appearance of Max and Carter that alarmed Lukas. It was Emilie, standing behind them and dressed in her own traveling cloak and pack. Where did she think she was going?

Lukas strode up to them, Paul frowning at his heels. "I see you two are ready for the road," he said, with a forced smile. "And, Emilie, are you planning to walk with us a ways to see us off?"

Emilie adjusted her pack, awkwardly, and planted her own walking stick firmly into the ground. "I'm coming with—"

"Don't say it."

She arched an eyebrow at him before completing her sentence, slowly and deliberately. Emilie did not like to be interrupted. "I'm coming with you."

"Emilie, this is not the time for stubborn-headed nonsense," whispered Lukas, and Paul let out an impressed whistle. Lukas had just called the Eldest Girl of the village stubborn-headed, but he didn't care. She was not going on this journey.

Emilie seemed to take the insult in stride and simply smoothed her cloak around her shoulders. "Since when did the Eldest Boy get to tell the Eldest Girl what to do?" she asked innocently.

"I'm in charge of the defense of this village," said Lukas.

"But this isn't a matter of defense," countered Emilie. "If I wanted to patrol the gate or hold a spear," she said, giving Max a sidelong glance, "you would be well within your right to forbid it. But this is an expedition outside the walls of our village, and there your authority ends. I'm going, too."

"And who will be Eldest Girl while you're gone?"

"Laura is the next oldest and is perfectly capable of handling things while I'm away, just as Finn will make a fine Eldest Boy in *your* absence."

"Look," said Lukas. "You've made your point. I know how you feel about Max holding that spear but this—"

"Do you really think me so petty?" said Emilie, and now her calm shell finally started to crack. "I am the Eldest Girl, and I have been since the first night, Lukas. The very first! I go where I please. Now lead on or stand aside. We're getting a late enough start as it is."

Paul let out another low whistle.

"And as for you, Paul," she said wheeling on the smirking boy. "My authority as Eldest Girl still stands so long as we are inside this village, so wipe that idiot grin off your face right now or I will switch your bottom red, here in front of everyone."

For once Paul made the smart choice, and his smile vanished. "Right. Sorry," he said, clearing his throat.

Lukas looked to Finn for help, but there was none to be found. Finn, indeed all the boys of the Watch, were studiously avoiding his gaze. Some had developed the sudden need to inspect their weapons while others just stared blankly at the dirt. He knew that any one of them would take a rat's dagger for their captain, but no one was willing to cross Emilie.

Max and Carter said nothing, although Max was wearing a curious expression. Was that satisfaction? She couldn't actually be pleased that Emilie wanted to go with them—the two girls had been at each other the wrong way since Max had arrived. But short of physically carrying Emilie back and locking her inside (which Lukas briefly considered), there was nothing he could do to prevent her from going with them. The best he could hope for was that she might come to her senses before they got too far for her to turn around.

"Fine," he said, turning his back to her. "I hope you packed your own food."

Lukas gave the signal, and the front gate groaned as it swung slowly open. Beyond, the Peddler's Road looked innocent and inviting. Just an ordinary road under a light morning mist. A pair of crows alighted on the gate, cocking their heads at the adventuring party.

"I wonder what they think about all this?" said Paul, glancing up at the black birds. "Probably going to have a good laugh at our expense."

"They're waiting for us to join arms and sing 'We're Off to See the Wizard,'" answered Max, but Lukas didn't have a chance to ask what she meant. Someone in the crowd was waving to him. A skinny plank of a boy was being helped along by two girls. But his cheeks were pink, and his eyes were clear, and the boy smiled at Lukas as he waved.

"Pidge," said Lukas. The boy was now up and about and recovering from his wounds. It was as good a sign as they were going to get.

And with that, the morning's gray thoughts, his doubts and his frustration with Emilie and his worries about what lay ahead, all vanished. The sun was up. Pidge was well again, and the journey before them felt a little less daunting than it had just a moment ago.

PART III

THE PEDDLER'S ROAD

CHAPTER EIGHTEEN

The rat known as Wormling had one talent that had kept him alive all these years. He wasn't large, nor was he fast or even particularly bright. But he'd reached an advanced age nearly unheard of among his kind because of a talent that had saved his tail time and again. It had gone so far as to make him valuable.

He was a good listener.

Not a listener in the sense that he was any kind of conversationalist; much the opposite. No one wanted to talk to Wormling for any length of time, not unless they wanted to hear about how many grubs he'd managed to squash with a stone that morning, or how many fleas he'd nibbled out of his fur the day before (old Wormling's hobbies were few, and all of them terribly dull).

No. No one wanted to talk to Wormling unless they needed information, unless he'd *listened* to something valuable being said. And this morning he'd definitely listened to something very valuable.

The two burly biters guarding the entrance to the mountain tunnel hissed at him as he slinked toward them. These two rats went by the names Spitter and Whiptail. Both were unpredictable brutes and bullies, and if Wormling didn't want his tail chewed off, he would need to be careful around them. So, as the old rat approached the tunnel to the main nest, he kept his ears flat against his head and his body low to the ground. Better to be submissive and let them know they were boss, at least for now, and keep his tail intact.

"What are you doing here?" snarled Spitter. "No mangy old flea sacks allowed near the females. Don't want the does to have to smell your stink."

"I'm delivering news," said Wormling. "Only news."

"Wait," said Whiptail. "I know you. You're that runt of a grub eater that sneaks around aboveground all day long. What is it they call you? Weirdling?"

"W-Wormling. They call me Wormling."

The rat barked out a harsh laugh. "Even better."

His partner bent down low and took one of Wormling's ears between his clawed fingers and gave it a harsh twist, causing the old rat to whimper. "What business do you have being aboveground all the time, anyway? You like being sunblind? You like smelling the flowers, is that it?"

"King Marrow orders it," said Wormling. At the mention of their leader's name, there was a change in the rat guards' breathing. It was subtle, but Wormling heard it. He'd been listening for it, and it sounded like fear.

"Maybe you tell me what Marrow has you doing up there and I'll let you keep this ear of yours, eh?" said Spitter, but then Whiptail rounded on him and slapped his companion across the snout with his tail. Fast as a whipcrack— Wormling could never have moved like that.

"Blast it!" cried Spitter, rubbing his snout. "What'd you do that for?"

"King Marrow's business is his own," snarled Whiptail. "You hear that, *Wormling*?" The big rat said Wormling's name with outright disgust. "We are minding our own here. You tell Marrow that when you see him. Pair of loyal rats, we are."

Then Whiptail shoved Wormling through the entrance and into the rat king's tunnel. Wormling stumbled and skinned himself against the rocky ground, but it was nice and dark down here and such a relief not to have to squint against the constant sunlight. The air was cool and moist, and the smell of rotting things made the rat hungry. Tunnel life seemed so luxurious to a poor creature like Wormling, who was used to very little.

It wouldn't do to linger here, though. Marrow would want Wormling's news as soon as possible, and yet Wormling did not press on right away. He made sure he was out of sight of the two guards, then crouched low against the tunnel's dirt wall and listened.

After a few minutes he heard one of them speak. It was in a low whisper, but Wormling's ears were very good.

"What'd you do that for, anyway?" Spitter was saying. "I should've twisted *your* ear off for that slap."

"And you're a flea-brained fool," answered Whiptail.

"That was Wormling, and whatever is said around Wormling always finds its way back to Marrow."

"What'd I say?"

"You were asking Marrow's business. The rat king keeps his business to himself, and those who go snooping find their tails chewed or worse."

"Bah," said Spitter. "Did you get a good look at Marrow the other night? He came back from New Hamelin in bad shape. All burned up, he was. Blind in one eye, they say. Not going to be running this nest much longer, not with wounds like that."

"Maybe," said Whiptail, sounding uncertain. *That was foolish,* thought Wormling. The rat would be better off defending their king. Much better off.

"I'm telling you," said Spitter. "Marrow will round a corner one of these days with that bad eye of his, and he won't see what's waiting there for him. *Who* is waiting there for him. There'll be a new king then, and he who's strong enough to take it can get all the food and all the does he wants."

"Well, I'm strong enough," said Whiptail. "But I'm not stupid enough. Marrow's a born killer, one eye or no. Still, I wouldn't mind seeing someone else try him. Wouldn't mind seeing that at all."

Wormling had listened to all that needed listening to. Slowly, quietly, he crept away. He'd heard that kind of talk many times before and usually paid it no mind. Rats said things when they were around other rats. Things they didn't really mean. Boasting, bragging. Empty threats. It was harmless talk to pass the time, and Wormling understood that. Usually.

Wormling knew he was getting close to the king's nest because he could smell the does, and something new—the scent of cooked fur.

The rats' war chief and ruler, King Marrow, was seated on a tall-backed chair of elvish design. Wormling didn't know how such a fine piece of furniture had found its way into Marrow's nest, but it was said that the skull Marrow used as a footrest had belonged to the chair's maker. Marrow was the largest rat Wormling had ever seen, maybe the largest these mountains had ever produced. He was a full head taller than the tallest New Hameliner, and he sat atop his chair like a human would, despite how uncomfortable or even painful it was for a rat to sit upright for so long. It was an unnatural posture for a rat, and yet Marrow almost always carried himself on two legs, as if he had something to prove to the New Hameliners in their village and the elves in their faraway forest: Rats could stand as tall as they, taller even. Marrow's meanness was rivaled only by his pride, and that's what made him such a strong leader. Many rats tried to emulate him; those two brutes Spitter and Whiptail had taken to walking upright. Not Wormling. It was safer to stay low to the ground.

But today their mighty leader looked miserable. The straw that padded the ground about him was filthy, and several does were tending to an angry red burn across Marrow's snout. It extended up his face and over his left eye, which was swollen shut. One female tried licking the wound, but Marrow let out a yelp and snapped at her, sending her scrambling for safety behind a line of waiting human children. The children stood at attention, holding trays of food for the rat king, but they kept their eyes downcast. A slave was the one creature more wretched than Wormling, and for a slave to look a rat in the eye could earn him a whipping.

"I don't need you worrying over me like some pink-skinned child," Marrow growled at the does. "Fetch me cool water. Now!"

The does retreated in a hurry, not sparing Wormling so much as a glance as they fled.

"Eh?" said Marrow, sniffing the air. "Who's that? Come closer, blast you."

His snout pressed to the ground, Wormling crawled forward.

"Wormling," said Marrow.

"Yes, my lord."

"I hope you've brought me good news," said Marrow. "I'm in a spiteful mood this morning."

"I did, my lord," said Wormling. His voice's natural pitch was a whine that set other rats' teeth on edge, he knew that. King Marrow flinched at it—yet another reason Wormling would have been killed long ago if not for his special talent for hearing things.

"And?"

"The crows are talking amongst themselves," said Wormling. "They are spilling secrets." With this, Wormling looked quizzically at the slaves. Marrow caught the old rat's meaning.

"Slaves, leave us," barked the rat king, and the children filed out of the king's nest in an orderly line. If they were relieved to be away from Marrow, and Wormling was sure they were, they didn't show it. They just walked quickly out, their heads hung low over the slave collars that they themselves had been made to forge. If Wormling had been a warmer creature, he might have pitied these captured children. It was said that Marrow sometimes took them aboveground on nights of the Winter's Moon, just so they could see the distant lights of their home village far away. Just to remind them that they would never get closer than that, not ever again.

Marrow was cruel, even for a rat, but that's why he was king.

After the last child had left, Marrow gestured to Wormling to come closer. "Now, tell me what you heard."

Wormling bowed. "The crows are talking about the new children that have arrived in the village, a girl and a boy."

"I know that!" snarled Marrow. "How do you think I got this?" he said, using a long claw to gesture to his ruined face. "Humans with their fires!"

"Of course, my lord," said Wormling. "Forgive me, my lord. But the crows are also saying something else. They say the boy has left the village."

Marrow's one good eye narrowed, and he sat forward on his haunches. "They say that, do they?"

"Set out today from New Hamelin, south on the Peddler's Road," said Wormling. "Along with his sister and three others. Packed for a long journey, too."

"Tell me," said Marrow. "Did the crows see a map? Were the Hameliners following a map?"

"If so, they did not say, my lord."

Wormling detected that an anxious note had crept into Marrow's voice at his mention of this map. It was not something Wormling was used to hearing there, which meant it could prove to be useful in the future. Wormling was an old creature, and Marrow hadn't been the first leader he'd served. Odds were he wouldn't be the last, either.

Marrow was looking directly at Wormling, but he wasn't really seeing him. The big rat's thoughts were elsewhere. "If they follow the road, they could run into the Peddler—that old magician is always walking it—he dare not leave. We'll need to find them first," he was saying, mostly to himself. "We can stop them at the troll bridge."

"Beyond the bridge, the Peddler's Road has grown treacherous, my lord," said Wormling. "I hear the Bonewood creeps closer every day, and the witch of that wood is always hungry."

Marrow grunted. "If *she* finds the children, there won't be anything left to deliver. We need to hurry."

Wormling thought that last bit was interesting. *Just who were they to deliver the children to?* he wondered. Another thing to tuck away inside his brain for later.

"I'll assemble a hunting party myself," said Marrow. "And I want you to come, too, Wormling. I'll want your ears."

Wormling nodded. The old rat hated journeys, and this smelled like a journey. But no one dared say no to King Marrow.

"And we'll need a few tough biters," said Marrow, thinking out loud again. "I can pull Spitter and Whiptail off guard duty."

"Ah, my lord?"

"You still here, Wormling?" asked Marrow. "What is it?"

"I beg your pardon," said Wormling, and he put on his

most apologetic whine, his most obsequious posture. He touched his sore ear and winced. Spitter had very nearly twisted it off. *All rats talked, but they needed to be careful about what they said. And they needed to be more careful which rats they decided to bully.*

"It's about Spitter and Whiptail, my lord," said Wormling. "I'm afraid I overheard them saying some rather unsavory things about Your Highness. Overheard by accident, of course. . . ."

As he told his story, Wormling wondered silently to himself whether Marrow would chew off only one of Spitter's ears or both.

It had been Tussleroot the First's own idea to cut across the Bonewood, though he regretted such foolishness now. Thus far, the Bonewood's fearsome appearance had matched its reputation, but Tussleroot's lone companion, Bandybulb, was turning out to be uncommonly brave for a fellow kobold. And being a king in exile, it wouldn't do for Tussleroot to look cowardly in front of his, as of yet, only subject.

Their intention had been to follow the Peddler's Road until they'd crossed the Western Fork. The lands between the river and the Deep Forest had grown too wild and too dangerous for kobolds, but the Peddler's Road would afford the two of them some protection on the journey. Wicked creatures did not like to stay on that road for long, lest they encounter the Peddler himself. The old magician wouldn't abide rats and ogres and witches using his road, but he was always a friend to kobolds and allowed them to come and go as they pleased, with his blessing and protection.

Tussleroot should've stayed on the road, but the shortcut had seemed like a tantalizingly quick and easy path to their destination. The sooner the kobolds reached the Shimmering Forest, the sooner Tussleroot could establish his new kingdom. Surely, once the other kobolds of that western forest saw him, they would flock to his banner. It would make no matter that they'd never heard of Tussleroot, and so what if there had never been a single king in all of kobold history? Loyal Bandybulb would sing such praises of Tussleroot the First that all would be convinced to give him a nice castle and a crown to replace his threadbare old hat. He might get to design his own flag.

Regardless, their old home in the midlands had grown too dangerous for a couple of fair-natured kobolds. The Princess now stayed locked in her castle, and the elves of the Deep Forest had burned all their bridges and closed their borders. Not even kobolds were welcome there anymore. It was a mean, spiteful thing for them to do, but when elves gave over to spite, they could be as fearsome as any ogres. Left unchecked by the elves, the Bonewood spread. The witch, it was said, now hunted here in the open. The rats dared to venture farther than ever, raiding and pillaging, and they grew bold enough to roam about in the daylight.

Best to pack up the kingdom (the contents of which fit snugly in a pole sack over Bandybulb's shoulder), say goodbye to their little copse of fir trees and make for fairer lands. No corner of the Summer Isle was completely untouched by the growing wickedness, and there were certainly rat problems out west, but the Shimmering Forest was as safe a place as any.

Thanks to Tussleroot's impatience, however, they had to make it through the Bonewood first. The forest, filled with ivory-hued trees as crooked as finger bones, had earned its name. High above, leaves the color of chalk choked out the sun, and down here, the forest floor was lightless and dreary as a grave. If Tussleroot hadn't known better, he would have said that those trees were not wood at all, but genuine bone. But bones didn't grow out of the earth, and bones didn't sprout leaves. At least, they shouldn't.

This forest was an unwholesome place that smelled of rotting vegetation and worse things. Tussleroot boasted to his good subject, Bandybulb, that he would've stayed and cleansed the place of evil if they hadn't been in such a hurry. But kingly duties awaited him.

They stopped at midday for a quick rest and a meal of cold beans and hard bread. Neither wanted to linger long enough to conjure up a fire.

"My lord?" said Bandybulb. "Is this shortcut going to take much longer?"

"Not much longer," answered Tussleroot, dubiously. "Just looking for a landmark." The elder kobold squinted at the trees around them. "Or a road sign," he added, under his breath.

Tussleroot chose not to acknowledge the obvious—that he'd gotten himself and his one and only subject lost. But it was the kobold's kingly philosophy that the more one ignores a thing, the less likely it is to be true. So instead, he busied himself with picking the brambles out of his fur with a broken-toothed comb.

The dim-witted Bandybulb munched on another mouthful of beans, a thoughtful expression on his face. An expression, suspected Tussleroot, that could only be for show.

"Do you think the stories are true, sire?"

"Hmm?" said Tussleroot. "What stories, good Bandybulb?"

"The crow stories," he said. "They say a boy and a girl have been found by the New Hameliners."

"You believe everything the crows tell you?" asked Tussleroot.

"Well, no, sire."

"And what do they say about Tussleroot the Magnificent, eh?" said Tussleroot. "You think Tussleroot cannot hear the crows' laughter as he passes by? You think that he does not know what they call him?"

"A knobby little potato with a hat for a crown and a dolt for a subject?"

Tussleroot smiled and patted the little kobold's cheek. "But a loyal dolt, Bandybulb. A loyal dolt."

"Yes, sire," said Bandybulb. "I know the crows are mostly full of stuff and nonsense. . . ."

"Utter nonsense. Tussleroot is clearly radish-shaped! Not like a potato at all."

"But they say a black tower has appeared in the north," persisted Bandybulb. "And now there are the new children—maybe the last ones. And they talk of the Piper. Ominous events, sire, if they're true."

Tussleroot stopped trying to untangle his matted fur and looked squarely at his subject. "If the crows speak truth, they still talk of things that do not concern us kobolds. You're too young to remember, but the Piper was locked away ages ago, and even before that, he took little interest in our kind. Were he free and up to mischief, then I reckon the Peddler and the Princess would deal with him, like they did the last time. Let the magicians sort it all out between themselves and let Tussleroot rule his people, er, person, in peace."

Satisfied that he'd just given a very kingly speech indeed, Tussleroot ordered Bandybulb to pack up their things. The shadows were getting long, and they'd overstayed their welcome in the Bonewood as it was.

The two hadn't marched much farther before they began to hear the sounds of distant crashes, like trees falling atop one another. Bandybulb scanned the trees with wide, frightened eyes. "Ogres?" he whispered.

"Most likely," said Tussleroot. "They wrestle each other for sport. But we will be safe as long as we move quietly and stay close to the ground. Ogres have trouble seeing below their fat bellies." Of course, an ogre could always step on you by accident, but Tussleroot saw no need to tell Bandybulb that.

They crept farther and farther through the forest. Tussleroot kept hoping that they would spot the Peddler's Road through the branches, yet all they saw were more and more skeletal trees. All the while, the smashing grew louder and closer. It seemed to be following them. If it really was wrestling ogres, they wouldn't follow a couple of little kobolds. They wouldn't even know how.

At Tussleroot's urging, they picked up their pace. No need to be quiet anymore, not with the racket of falling trees crashing around them. All there was left to do was to run.

As the two kobolds broke through a patch of thornbushes, they saw it—the trees thinning up ahead and, beyond, a long stretch of open road. It was within sight—if only the two could make it there in time.

Then a shadow passed over their heads as something massive stepped over them. A giant foot, clawed and four-toed like a chicken's, placed itself in their path. Another foot landed behind them, and atop those two enormous feet were legs as tall as trees. And atop them, there rested a dingy old hut. Skulls dangled from the hut's roof like wind chimes, and a noxious green smoke poured forth from a squat chimney. Tussleroot threw himself to the ground and scrambled inside a hollow rotted log. If there was one thing kobolds were, they were good hiders.

"Bandybulb!" Tussleroot whispered, looking around for his companion. But then he heard the kobold shouting. Tussleroot poked his head out of the log and saw his subject, loyal, half-brained Bandybulb, brandishing a stick in both hands like a sword and charging at the giant clawed foot.

"I will defend you, sire!" the little kobold was shouting. "Long live the—"

The kobold's words were lost as the second foot reached forward and plucked up Bandybulb between its toes. The foot lifted him high into the air, and in the storm of falling dirt and leaves, Tussleroot was forced to look away.

Then a high-pitched cackle, a laugh of obscene delight, rang forth from inside the hut, and the monstrous thing turned and stomped away, horrible chicken legs and all. It disappeared into the Bonewood.

Tussleroot cowered there in his hiding spot for what seemed like hours, looking for the courage to move again. Slowly he crawled along the forest floor until he was back on the road, back to safety. There was no sign of Bandybulb, and Tussleroot hadn't bothered to search the broken trees for the poor kobold. He knew where Bandybulb had been taken, and he knew what sort of creature had taken him.

So Tussleroot the First, the king without a kingdom, fled the forest of witches and ogres and made for safer lands. Alone.

CHAPTER NINETEEN

The morning's journey started out well. Although the Peddler's Road led through the Shimmering Forest, the path was wide, and mostly clear of overhanging branches. It was as if the trees of the forest were keeping a respectful distance from the magician's road. From what Carter could see of the wood, it looked pleasant enough, though Paul assured him that there were dangers even in a relatively friendly forest such as this. The shimmering lights that gave the forest its name could lead unwary travelers astray, he cautioned, and a person could get lost for days or longer. But here on the road, Carter and his friends were safe, and the sky above was a startling blue, and the bright sun banished the drifting fairy lights to seek the shade of deeper parts of the forest.

By midday, Carter's stomach was rumbling like thunder and his leg ached terribly. Lukas had called for them to slow their pace several times, but Carter had always protested. He was as fit for this journey as any of them. He'd prove it.

Carter had never been what one might call an outdoor kid. It was easier in many ways to live in the pixilated world of computers and the magical forests of role-playing games than to endure the chiggers, hay fever and mosquito bites that came with real-world nature. That, and it was easier to go hiking when you didn't need someone to hold your hand so you didn't trip on the trail. No, Carter's own forests were limited only by his own imagination, and in those fantasies he was as strong and as fast as anybody. Faster even. The trees could be bright purple and seventy feet tall, and Carter could be a level-eighteen paladin in full plate armor, wielding a +10 broadsword of fire, all the while sitting in his room with the thermostat set to a comfortable seventy-two degrees.

Here on the Summer Isle, things were different. Although he certainly wasn't dressed in plate armor, wearing a cloak around his neck and a knife at his belt did make him feel like an adventurer. This wasn't camp or some boring nature walk. Yes, he already had blisters, and he'd hiked half the day with a stitch in his side. And though there weren't any mosquitoes that he could see, they were occasionally ambushed by these little green-winged moths that wanted nothing better than to fly up your nose.

Yet Carter couldn't remember a time when he'd been happier. He was on a quest. An actual quest, with a brave band of heroes set out to save the kingdom. Or a group of kids set out to save the village, at least. It was still the stuff of daydreams, and he was glad that Max could be here to share in this one. If she'd only let herself enjoy it a little.

And if his sister refused to have any fun, then she darn well better let him carry the spear.

They finally stopped to eat lunch beneath a tall, twisted tree Paul called a ropewood tree. The boughs were actually made up of two or three smaller ones that grew around and around each other, giving the long, curling branches the ropelike appearance for which the tree was named. Paul warned them that in meaner forests, these trees were called hangman's trees, and you'd never want to stop for lunch near one of those. Everyone scooted just a few feet closer to the road after hearing that.

That was how this world was, thought Carter. A place similar to the real world in so many ways, except . . . wilder. Fiercer. The flowers could make you heady, their scents were so strong, and the forests loomed over everything, watchful. The sun was brighter in the sky, and the nights, when they came, were darker and more terrifying.

At lunchtime, Carter discovered that the delicacies of last night's feast were not on today's menu. Instead, they dined on travel rations—hard bread, a handful of dried fruit and more of that tough-as-leather salted pork. When Carter was forced to give up on his pork for fear of losing a tooth, Paul happily took his share. And Max said *Carter* had a bottomless stomach.

As for the rest of their party of adventurers, Max ate her lunch in silence while Lukas and Emilie sat on opposite sides of their little camp, each avoiding the other. With no one to talk to, Carter lay back and contented himself with staring into the forest. Twinkling lights had begun to appear in the distance and flitted between the branches. Some looked as big as a person's head. Carter was watching them drift among the leaves when a boy suddenly appeared. He was smiling and laughing as he chased the lights through the trees.

Carter sat up quickly and squinted to get a better look. Was the boy a New Hameliner? Something about the light in the forest made him look blurry around the edges. Carter was just getting ready to call for Max when the boy vanished. Carter blinked and rubbed his eyes, but the boy was really gone.

Paul drifted over to his side. "You saw him, too?"

Carter nodded. He hadn't imagined it, at least. "Who was he?"

"Don't know," said Paul. "You see things in the wild, especially here in the Shimmering Forest. Those lights can play tricks on your eyes. Or he may have been a ghost. We get those, too, from time to time, though it's rare to see one wandering this far inland. There's a village down on the coast called Shades Harbor that's thick with them."

"Ghosts?" Back when Lukas had interrogated Carter, one of the first things he'd asked was if Carter was a ghost. So much had happened since then that Carter had forgotten all about the strange question. "So, there's ghosts on the Summer Isle, too?"

"Some are true ghosts, passing through to the other side," said Paul. "Others are just dreamers. Those ones are only visiting. I think they take a wrong turn in their dreams and end up here for a spell. Can be hard to tell them apart, though."

"And you said there's a whole village of them?"

Paul leaned close and whispered. "I've seen it. Big black ships bringing the shades to shore. Ghosts and dreamers wandering lost. It's a lonely place."

"I don't think I like the sound of that."

Paul shook his head. "Then there's others still, worse ones. . . . But I don't like to talk about any of them. Stay clear of them all, I say."

"He looked so real," said Carter.

"You've gotta trust more than just your eyes when you're out here in the wild," said Paul, with a devilish grin.

Carter scanned the forest once more, hoping to catch another glimpse of the smiling boy, but he was truly gone. *Was he a dreamer?* Carter wondered. Carter hoped the boy was really safe and snug in his bed somewhere. To him this place would have been just another part of the dream—a dream of chasing fireflies. Or was the boy someone's spirit, and if so, where was he going?

"Why don't you tell me about your home?" said Paul, interrupting Carter's train of thought. He was no longer concerned with the boy in the woods, and why should he be? He was a scout, their guide through this magical land, and all this was just a part of his every day. "I overheard you and your sister talking about it—someplace called Greenwich Village."

Paul stuffed a hunk of dried pork in between his cheek and gum, like a chipmunk.

"Well," said Carter. "What do you want to know?"

"Does Greenwich Village have a wall like New Hamelin does?"

"Oh, well, no. And people just *call* it Greenwich Village. It's actually part of a big city called New York."

"A city?" repeated Paul, sounding impressed. "A village inside of a city! I can't imagine it. Do they have great big manor houses there? Say, did you grow up in a castle?"

"No, we live in a third-floor walk-up."

Paul shook his head. "Ah, too bad. I always wanted to know what it was like to live in a castle. They say the Princess lives in one, though I've never seen it."

"Sorry."

Paul leaned back and put his arms behind his head so he could look up at the branches of the ropewood tree. "If I lived in a castle, I'd make a really good king, you know. I'd order my subjects to hunt and play all day long. No work whatsoever. Then we'd eat until we passed out in our chairs. Really good king, don't you think?"

"Sure," lied Carter. King Paul would be really good for about a week, until people realized nothing was getting done.

"Did you have a trade in Greenwich Village? I'm a scout, which is by far the best thing to be, though I think I was once apprenticed to a tailor. Can't remember, really. What did you do?"

"Uh, well I went to school. And my dad's a teacher, so I guess that's a trade. Kind of."

Paul sat up and squinted at Carter for a moment. "You remember what he looked like?" he asked. "Your father?"

"Well, yeah," said Carter.

"That's lucky," said Paul. "You're lucky, Carter."

"Yeah." Carter didn't really know what else to say. It was one of the saddest things he'd ever heard—so many children in New Hamelin and so few memories.

"Well," said Carter, looking for something else to talk

about. "Do you think we might run into him? The Peddler, I mean."

Paul shrugged. "Maybe. He's always on the road, but you never know where. Always traveling. Strange old fellow, anyhow. If we miss him, you're not missing much, in my opinion. Don't know why everyone makes such a big deal—"

Their conversation was interrupted by the distinctive snap of a twig nearby. Paul was suddenly alert, his head cocked and listening. The snapping twig was followed by the rustling of leaves. At first Carter feared that the sounds were coming from the ropewood itself, that the tree was coming to life to hang them all. But it soon became obvious that the branches weren't moving on their own. Something was moving in them.

Lukas saw it now, too, and one of his hands went to his lips to gesture for quiet while the other reached for his hatchet. Paul had begun to quietly yet quickly string his bow. Even Max had taken up her spear, though her hands fidgeted as if she wasn't sure how to hold it. Carter drew his tiny knife and stared up into the branches. Something was moving up there, and it was . . . giggling?

Lukas let out a long sigh of relief. "It's all right," he said softly, and lowered his hatchet.

"But what is it?" asked Max.

"Kobolds!" answered Paul, breaking out into a huge grin. "Brilliant!" He reached for his quiver.

"We are not wasting arrows on woodland sprites," said Emilie.

"They'll be wanting to play," said Paul, with obvious disappointment.

"And we are not going to encourage them," said Emilie.

"Where?" asked Carter. "I can't see them."

"Kobolds are good at hiding," said Emilie. "But they are all mischief makers."

"And they think it's fun to have someone shoot arrows at them?" asked Max.

"Came close to hitting one once," answered Paul, nodding. "But they are quick as lightning."

Lukas hefted his pack up off the ground. "Arrows can't hurt them," he said. "But Emilie's right. Even kobolds can be troublesome if they get riled up. We need to get a move on, anyway."

While the rest of them gathered their things, Carter kept peering into the tree overhead. Every now and then laughter would burst forth from the branches—a whole chorus of tiny voices now—but he still couldn't see anything.

As they left the shade of the ropewood tree and set out again on the road, Carter spared one last look back. The branches were absolutely quivering with movement now. The leaves began to part, and Carter saw . . . butts. Scores of fat little behinds, poking out through the branches and wiggling in his direction. Carter stopped in his tracks, unsure if he was really seeing what he was seeing.

"Will you look at that!" said Paul, stopping beside him. "Nasty little creatures, aren't they?" Then Paul made as if he was drawing back his bowstring and let an imaginary arrow fly. The kobolds cheered.

Carter's first adventure, the first day of his great quest, and he'd just been mooned.

CHAPTER TWENTY

Max didn't sleep at all that evening on the road, and the next several days weren't much better. Even though Lukas and Paul took turns keeping a watch in the evenings, what little sleep Max could come by was restless and troubled. Exhaustion finally began to catch up with her as her whole body had begun to ache and her thoughts turned muddy and thick. She couldn't stomach breakfast, but what she would have given for a cup of coffee.

The Shimmering Forest went on forever, but while the trees seemed unending and unchanging, the Peddler's Road itself underwent a significant transformation. The dirt road that they'd been following gave way to a cobblestone highway, lined with lonely ivy-covered arches that appeared every half mile or so. Paul told them that this once grand stretch of road had been the Peddler's gift to the Princess of the Elves, dedicated to her. But that was long ago, in happier times, and now it was little more than a ruin in the wild, overgrown with vines.

The constant summer sun climbed high overhead, but rather than cool the road with their shade, the trees seemed to trap the heat in while blocking out any breezes that might have offered relief. Max's armored vest grew heavy and the shirt beneath soaked through with sweat, but it didn't seem worth the energy to take the vest off, especially since she wasn't about to ask someone to carry it for her.

It was a relief when they finally stopped to rest in the shade of a tall willow tree on the bank of a pond. The pond was lovely and covered in blooming lily pads with dragon-flies that fluttered in and among the petals. Lukas agreed that they could stop there for a brief rest, though he cautioned everyone that this might be a nixie pond and to stay away from the water's edge. Max had no idea what that meant, and she was too tired to ask. Still, it felt good to stop moving, if only for a few minutes, and Max allowed herself to close her eyes. She waved away the offer of food and wanted nothing more than to lie in the cool grass. Her head was swimming and the thought of eating made her feel sick, anyway.

"When was the last time you really slept?" asked Emilie, giving her shoulder a little nudge.

Max couldn't believe she had only just closed her eyes and already this girl was shaking her awake.

"Can't I just rest for ten minutes?" asked Max.

"I said, when was the last time you really slept?"

Max bit back a nasty retort—she'd be asleep now if Emilie would just leave her alone. Confusion and sickness were symptoms of sleep deprivation, Max knew. And so, apparently, was irritability. "I'll be fine," said Max, yawning.

"You silly girl, I didn't ask if you would be fine," said Emilie. "I asked when was the last time you slept."

Max sat up and glared at her. Why did every word out of her mouth sound like it was coming from some nineteenth-century school governess? Nevertheless, Max couldn't find the strength to argue.

"I don't know," she answered instead. "Guess I just miss my pillow."

"You need to take care of your body, or it will fail you," said Emilie.

"Look, I just need a catnap and then I'll be good to go."

"Just so," answered Emilie. Someone had already built a small campfire while Max had been resting. Balanced atop the flames was a small cast-iron pot, which Emilie carefully picked up using her skirt. She poured steaming water into a small wooden cup and handed it to Max. "I had them make a fire so I could brew you this special tea. Drink it all, down to the dregs, and it will restore some of your strength. But tonight you must sleep. I can brew you a different tea to help with that if need be."

Max remembered the last time Emilie had offered her tea. It had led to an argument. She'd been wondering if it was something said during that argument that had convinced Emilie to come with them.

"Fine. Thanks."

"Don't thank me," said Emilie. "Drink my tea."

Max sipped at the hot liquid—it was a bit flowery for her taste but wasn't all bad. Her cup in hand, Max found her brother sitting by the pond and trying to teach himself to whittle with his little knife.

"What are you making?" asked Max.

Carter looked at his handiwork. "I was going to turn this twig into a dog, but I think this is just going to end up a smaller twig—hey, did you see that?"

Her brother pointed to the pond where, if Max squinted, she could see several of the lily pads bobbing up and down in the water. It looked like something, or several somethings, was swimming just below the surface. Whatever they were, they were big.

"You think those are those nixie things Lukas was warning us about?" asked Max.

Carter nodded, excitedly. "Nixies are water spirits. They appear in all sorts of stories, but they aren't usually dangerous."

"They aren't," said Lukas, joining their conversation. "But where there are nixies, there might also be nokks."

"What's a nokk?" asked Max.

"Male water spirits," answered Lukas, staring at the pond fearfully. "They appear as old men with seaweed hair, and they lurk at the bottom of ponds and rivers. Like most wicked things, they can't abide the light, but if you swim too deep, they will grab your ankles and pull you under."

"Do you think there's a nokk in there?" asked Carter. For some reason, the possibility seemed to excite him even more.

"I don't know," said Lukas. "But if you ever do see one, there's a little charm to ward him off. Say his name three times—*nokk, nokk, nokk.*"

"Who's there?" said Max, but Lukas just blinked at her, expressionless. "Sorry, bad joke."

"Of course," continued Lukas. "You can't say his name if your lungs are full of water, so it's best we stay clear of the pond altogether. I can't think of anything worse than drowning. I've never liked the water. I don't like not knowing what's in there with me."

"No problem," said Max. "It's good to know that something scares you. I was beginning to feel like a coward around all of you."

"Plenty of things scare me," said Lukas. "But as a member of the Watch, you try to control your fears, because in this place, the dark has a way of making fears come to life."

"If you're trying to reassure me, you're doing a terrible job," said Max.

"We'll be fine in the daytime," said Lukas.

"And if we're still out here on a true night, when the sun goes down?"

Lukas glanced at Max's brother, but he didn't answer Max's question. "Come on," he said. "Paul's back."

"Back?" said Max. She hadn't known that Paul had ever left.

"You've been napping for hours," said Carter. "Emilie said you looked like you needed it."

Max felt the color rise to her cheeks. She thought she'd been asleep for a few minutes at the most. No wonder Emilie had poked her awake.

They returned to their camp, where Paul and Emilie were already kicking dirt over their small fire.

"We might need to do without a fire this evening," said Emilie. "Paul thinks we are being followed."

"Followed?" said Carter. "Is it the kobolds?"

Paul shook his head. "They're too big to be kobolds. They're using the road, same as us, and they're moving fast. I only spotted them because Lukas asked me to do some scouting of the woods while Max was sleeping. I think it's safe to assume they've seen the smoke from our fire." Max felt her blush deepen even more because they'd only made that fire so Emilie could brew tea for her.

"It could be rats," said Lukas. "Probably a scavenger party."

"I could try to get a closer look if you want," said Paul.

"No," said Emilie. "No more running off by your lonesome. We keep together from here on out."

Max watched Lukas's face. Emilie had just taken hold of the conversation, giving orders where it had been Lukas's place. But if he resented it, he didn't let it show, on his face at least. Max thought she detected a hint of annoyance in his voice when he next spoke, and she found it reassuring that she wasn't the only one who had to bite her tongue around Emilie.

"Paul, what's the road like ahead?" Lukas asked.

"It bends to the east about a mile or so on. Then it's pretty much a straight line until the river."

"Wait a minute," said Max. "I thought the rats only came out at night?"

"That's when the packs do," said Lukas.

"Mischiefs," said Carter.

"Pardon?" said Lukas.

"Oh, uh, a group of rats is called a *mischief,* not a pack," Carter said. "I read it somewhere."

Now was hardly the time for a vocabulary lesson, but Carter sometimes couldn't resist showing off that big brain of his. Max was used to it, but Lukas and the rest were getting their first taste.

"All right, then," said Lukas. "The mischiefs come out at night, but sometimes we see a few of them during the day. And we can avoid them, if we're smart."

"So what do we do?" asked Carter.

Lukas reached into his belt and withdrew his leather scroll case. It gleamed in the sunlight, as the leather had been oiled to keep moisture out. Inside, carefully protected, was the Peddler's map.

He carefully unrolled it on the ground in front of them. "We can leave the road here," he said, pointing to a section of map that lay between the dotted line of the road and a river. Someone had sketched in little boulders and trees and a little arched bridge. There were words written next to the bridge, but they were too small for Max to read over Lukas's shoulder. "If we cut through the forest, we can make camp and be off the road while the rats pass us by."

"Are you sure that's the best plan?" asked Max. "What if these rats decide to leave the road, too? What if they find us?" She gave Lukas a pointed look to remind him of his promise to her—the promise to keep Carter safe.

Lukas looked Max in the eye. "If they do, it'll be the worse for them. If it comes to a fight, Paul and I can handle a couple of rats."

Paul let out a twanging sound and made as if he was aiming his bow, a sly grin on his face. "Better than wasting arrows on kobolds."

"Boys," said Emilie with an exasperated sigh. "Always confusing fighting for playing." For once, Max couldn't have agreed more.

"It's settled, then," said Lukas. "We leave the road and head east to the river."

"Awesome," said Carter, her brother's cheerfulness undaunted by the nixies, nokks or even giant rats. It was annoying.

CHAPTER TWENTY-ONE

Carter dreamed he was walking through an autumn wood. Golden-red colors fell around him as leaves fluttered by on a cool breeze. The forest floor crunched beneath his feet. Someone was whistling a tune nearby.

He couldn't find his companions, but Max wouldn't have let him wander off by himself, surely. With no better options, Carter decided to follow the music. The whistler might be his sister, or if not, at least he could ask directions. To where exactly, he wasn't sure, but he knew he needed to get somewhere.

The whistler turned out to be the ratcatcher, dressed in his starched white uniform and cap, and sitting on a moss-covered log. He was using Carter's knife to whittle a piece of wood, and whistling while he worked. Carter couldn't place the song, though the tune sounded familiar. The words

Pest Control were stitched across the front of his cap in bright red letters that seemed to shift and bleed when Carter stared at them for too long.

"Hello, Carter," said the ratcatcher without looking up from his work.

"I know you," said Carter. "I shouldn't be talking to you."

"Now you sound like your sister," said the ratcatcher. "How is she, by the way? Is she sleeping yet? I haven't seen her around here."

"Emilie gave her some tea to help her sleep," said Carter, remembering. "The stuff knocked her right out. Maybe that's why I can't find her, either."

"Ah, that explains it," said the ratcatcher, pausing in his knife work. "One of Emilie's home-brewed potions. Your sister won't be dreaming tonight."

Carter felt like he should be alarmed at seeing the ratcatcher here in the forest. It was something to warn the others about, at least, but seeing as the others were nowhere around, there wasn't anyone to tell. If he ran from the ratcatcher or told him to go away, then he would be alone, and Carter did not want to be alone.

"What do you think?" said the ratcatcher, holding up the stick he'd been working on. "Nearly finished with this one."

The stick was no longer just a stick; it was now very nearly a small flute. Rough along one end, where the wood was still splintered and raw, but the finger holes were evenly spaced and the mouthpiece looked smooth. Carter wondered how he'd managed to hollow the thing out with nothing but Carter's tiny knife.

"What are you going to do with it?" asked Carter.

"Play music, of course," said the ratcatcher. "But it'll never be as good as my old one." The ratcatcher shook his head wistfully. "In the meantime, I'd like to give you a little advice—you're wasting your time with your friends, Carter. You don't need them. But I can help you, if you'll let me." Finally, the ratcatcher looked up, and Carter got a clear look at his face. It was familiar, as familiar as the song he'd been whistling.

That face. If Carter could stare at it for just a few more seconds, he was sure he could place it. It was very, very important that he did.

"Whoops," said the ratcatcher. "Time to go. Just remember that the rats are afraid of the water."

Then he smiled. "I taught them to be."

Carter woke with a start, and at first he was afraid he'd simply woken into another dream. He was still looking at trees, but these trees were lush with the green leaves of summer. When he sat up and squinted in the dim morning light, he was startled to see a figure perched near him, sitting on a moss-covered log.

"Wake up," said Paul, nudging him with his toe.

"Oh," said Carter. "Good morning."

"We've got a visitor," said Paul, pointing.

Carter sat up and rubbed his eyes. A few yards away, Lukas was huddled in conversation with what looked like a small hairy man. He was maybe a foot and a half tall, plump, and dressed in dingy overalls and a little hat. His clothing was filthy and worn thin, and tufts of hair poked through at the seams.

"Is that . . . ," said Carter, trying to shake himself awake. "Wait, what is that?"

"A kobold," answered Paul. "But he doesn't look like much fun. If I loosed an arrow at him, he'd probably turn me into a toad."

"Wow," said Carter. Last night's dream and all its grim portents disappeared with the sight of the furry little man in a hat.

Lukas straightened up and walked back to their camp. The kobold followed. Emilie was awake now and pulling out bits of forest that had settled in her hair overnight. Some leaves, a bug or two.

"This is His Majesty Tussleroot," said Lukas. "He's, uh, king here."

"From that tree," said the kobold, pointing, "to this rock. Tussleroot's kingdom is vast."

Carter looked down at the ground they'd been sleeping on. The shortcut through the forest was taking longer than any of them had expected, and it was especially hard on Carter's bad leg. The hidden ditches and patches of loose earth made the way treacherous, and stones kept getting lodged between Carter's leg brace and his foot. After nearly a day of slogging across this unforgiving ground, they'd made camp in this clearing. Visible now in the bright morning sunlight was a ring of toadstools that circled the area where they'd been sleeping. The toadstools apparently marked the outlines of the kobold's kingdom—a circle approximately five feet in diameter.

"I was just explaining that we meant no disrespect in setting up camp here," said Lukas. "And that we are, uh, weary travelers seeking safety in his . . . lands."

Tussleroot hooked his thumbs into the straps of his overalls and nodded magnanimously. "Tussleroot forgives your transgression and hereby grants you safe passage through his kingdom. No harm shall come to you while you are within its borders."

The way Carter was sitting, his left foot was already sticking well past those borders. Were he to scoot a little to the left or right, he'd be out of them entirely.

"We thank his majesty for his generosity," said Emilie, with a meaningful look back at Carter and Paul. "Don't we?"

"Huh?" said Paul. "Oh, yeah. But where are all your people?"

"Tussleroot has only ever had one subject, and he was lost. Now there is only Tussleroot." Tussleroot bowed his head for a moment before looking up at them slyly. "Say, you aren't in need of a king, are you?"

"No, I'm sorry," said Carter. He'd been waiting for Max to say something snarky when he realized that his sister was still sleeping. She was huddled up in a little ball and snoring softly.

"I was just telling Tussleroot about the rats on the road, and he says that he's seen them before," said Lukas.

"They are cruel, but would not dare cross Tussleroot's borders."

Paul barely stifled a laugh, and Carter couldn't blame him. It would take about two steps to circumvent Tussleroot's kingdom entirely.

"He thinks they are still on the road, though," said Lukas. "Between us and the river."

"Big rats," said Tussleroot, nodding. "Rats usually steer clear of the Peddler's Road, so they must be searching for someone. Maybe you, Tussleroot is thinking."

That didn't sound good. Carter didn't see how they could risk getting back on the road now.

"Tussleroot, is there a safe path through the woods to the river?" asked Emilie. "We need to cross the Western Fork and avoid the rats, but we're having trouble finding our way."

Tussleroot scratched his furry chin. "Tussleroot knows a path. Then you could follow the river south to the troll bridge. But you shouldn't. The lands to the east have grown very dangerous. Even along the Peddler's Road. Very dangerous."

"We'll be careful," said Lukas.

"Troll bridge?" whispered Carter, but Emilie waved him into silence.

"We appreciate the warning, your majesty," said Emilie. "But we must go there nonetheless, and we appreciate any help you can give us."

With that, they began gathering up their things while Tussleroot looked on disapprovingly. Astoundingly, Max kept on snoring through it all. Emilie explained that the tea she'd given her the night before might make waking her difficult and that at the very least she was sure to be groggy. Carter thought this was probably for the best, because he could hardly imagine his sister's reaction when she found out where they were headed next.

❧ CHAPTER TWENTY-TWO ❧

Despite the little kobold's inflated sense of self, Lukas was grateful for Tussleroot's help. He guided them out of the forest, and they reached the riverbank by midafternoon. The Great River split the Summer Isle into halves, and the river's arms were called the Forks. The Western Fork was sluggish, muddy and deep, while the Eastern Fork was shallow and fast and clear as ice water.

After bidding goodbye to his majesty King Tussleroot the First, Lukas and his companions followed the Western Fork south. Paul and Carter skipped rocks along the water's edge while Emilie lectured Max on the dangers of overexerting oneself. Poor Max, thought Lukas, but at least it kept Emilie too busy to lecture *him* on any number of other things.

As they hiked along the riverbank, Lukas absently fingered the map case in his belt, thinking of the little dotted line they were following and where it went. The Peddler's Road cut across both forks, winding all the way past the Deep Forest and onward to the sea. They'd need to leave the road before then, and march the rest of the way north across the moors to find the Black Tower. And there were doubtless many dangers between here and there. The isle only got wilder the farther east one traveled.

And yet, Lukas's heart felt lighter than it had in a long, long time, since before he'd inherited the title of Eldest Boy, since he had become responsible for defending a village of over a hundred children. The backpack strapped to his shoulders wasn't nearly as heavy as the Iron Sword, not when weighed in duty. He'd even found the time to join Paul and Carter in a game of skipping stones. Lukas hadn't lost his knack for finding the best-shaped rocks. They needed to be flat, of course, but not so thin that they didn't have any momentum, because a good skipping stone also needed to be heavy enough to go far.

Lukas probably should've been more worried, especially with the rats nearby, but it was hard not to get caught up in the freedom of the adventure. Of course he'd honor his promise to Max by keeping her brother safe, and together he truly believed they would reach the Black Tower and, hopefully, find the way home. And if not, if the prophecy turned out to be false, well, then Lukas had a secret plan for that, too. Because he wasn't going back to New Hamelin, at least not as Eldest Boy. If he returned at all, he'd refuse to take back the sword from Finn. Lukas was done with it.

After less than an hour's walk, they spotted what they

were looking for—the oddly shaped stone arch known as the troll bridge. It spanned the Western Fork from one bank of the river to the other, and the Peddler's Road, which emerged from the trees a few leagues to the south, went right up to the bridge's foot. The road continued again on the far bank. Except for the many wrens nesting there, the bridge was empty. Not another soul in sight.

"So that's it?" asked Max as they drew nearer. "That's the troll bridge?"

Lukas nodded, suppressing a smile. He knew what the next question would be. In fact, he'd been looking forward to it.

"So where's the troll?" asked Carter. The boy actually looked ready to run on ahead until Max yanked him back by the hood of his cloak. Carter was brave enough to be called foolhardy.

"That's the troll," answered Lukas, pointing at the bridge.

"Where?" asked Max. "Under the bridge?"

"No," said Lukas, unable to stifle his laughter any longer. "It *is* the bridge. Look closer. Go on, I promise it's safe."

Max's forehead scrunched up in confusion—she wasn't enjoying this little game. But as she took a few steps closer, her eyes grew wide. Lukas should've prepared them for the truth, but this way was easier than explaining. And, honestly, it was so much more fun.

"Really, Lukas," said Emilie. "You're almost as bad as Paul."

The thing about the troll bridge was, if you looked at any single section, you'd think it was just a poorly chiseled bridge of lumpy rock laid across the river. But when one stood back and took in the structure as a whole, the truth gradually revealed itself. The bridge began on the near bank with a great clawed foot, its toes having buried themselves into the earth long ago. That foot's leg was wholly submerged beneath the water, but the other leg rose up out of the waves and spanned half the river before joining a fat-bellied waist and chest. One side of the head cleared the water's surface, and one enormous crooked arm stretched up and over, all the way to the far bank. The whole thing looked like an enormous stone giant crawling across the river on all fours, which was exactly what it had been.

"It looks like a giant statue fell across the river," said Max.

"It's a giant troll, actually," said Lukas. "A very *unlucky* giant troll who found himself caught at dawn crossing the Fork. Sun came up, and the troll did what trolls do in the sunlight. He's been that way ever since, and now we have ourselves a stone bridge."

"Nice of him to place himself so conveniently," said Paul.

"Show a little respect," chided Emilie.

Once Lukas had assured Max that it was safe, they let Carter take the lead. "No way!" he said, coming to a stop at the troll's stony foot. Several of the giant's toes had broken off long ago, and in the years since, the wind and rain had transformed them into freestanding boulders.

Lukas joined him and brushed his fingers across one of the rocky toes. Time had smoothed out the troll's bumpy skin, and a ledge of toadstools now grew over the toenail. *Some things do get older,* he thought to himself. *Just not us.*

"It's amazing," said Max. "How long has this been here?"

"Longer than we have," answered Lukas.

"Once there were many trolls that roamed the Summer Isle," said Emilie. "But most have gone to sleep, as this one has. Trolls never stop growing, you see, and it becomes hard to escape the sun when you get so very big. And this fellow was comparatively small."

"So, are you saying that there are even bigger ones?" asked Carter. "Are they stone, too?"

Emilie nodded. "As we journey on, keep a look out for an oddly shaped hill or a lonely mountain. It might have been a troll once upon a time."

Paul let out a fake snore. "Boring. Are we crossing anytime soon?"

Lukas gave the other boy a playful slap to the back of his head. They were far from the village, but if Paul wasn't careful, Emilie would swat his backside right here in the middle of the wild. Lukas wouldn't put it past her.

"All right, follow me and watch your step. That river's a cold swim," said Lukas, and he began climbing up the great stone leg. "Paul, you keep an eye on our backs."

The path across the bridge would be slow going. Lukas eyed the river warily. He hadn't been totally honest when he'd told Max that he didn't like the water. The truth was, it terrified him. A shallow stream or clear pool where he could see the bottom didn't bother him, but murky lakes and muddy rivers made Lukas's mouth go dry with fear. Too much space down there for something to hide.

Still, there was no other way across the Western Fork,

not for miles at least, so they carefully made the climb together. Max helped her brother along, taking special care at points where the stone was the most perilous, and Lukas kept their pace slow so the boy could keep up. They were lucky that there hadn't been any heavy rains of late, but even so, patches were slick with river moss, and once Emilie lost her footing and nearly slid into the water. It was Paul who actually threw out a hand to steady her, much to the girl's chagrin.

They were three quarters of the way across when Max asked, "What if the rats are already ahead of us? Are you looking for tracks?"

"No," said Lukas. "But I know who to ask."

Max gave him a confused look. "You planning on meeting someone?"

"Watch," said Lukas. Soon they came to the place he'd been looking for. Partly submerged, half the troll's ancient stone face peered up from the water. His eyes were closed, and his expression peaceful—a slumbering giant of stone. They picked out a path across the troll's rocky neck until they found its enormous ear, the canal of which had become a nesting place for a family of wrens.

"Emilie," said Lukas. "You are probably better at this part than I am."

"Give me a hand up," she said. "And so help me, Lukas, if I fall into that river, you will regret it for the next hundred years."

Lukas nodded that he understood—Emilie did not make idle threats—and kept one hand on her arm to steady her.

Together they scrambled up the pockmarked and weather-worn earlobe. The wrens, after much squawking and carrying on, took flight.

Lukas heard Carter asking Paul what was going on, but the scout just shushed him. Even the prankster knew that this was serious work they were about to attempt.

Emilie leaned low and, cupping her hand around her mouth, she began to whisper into the troll's ear. She hadn't been flippant in her choice of words when she said the trolls slept. Their bodies turned to stone in the sun and they rejoined the earth from which they were made, but they could be woken up, somewhat. It was possible, if you knew the right words, to stir them just enough to have a chat. The trick was not to disturb them so much that they felt the need to roll over.

Soon there was a low rumble from deep beneath their feet, a rumble that became words and gurgled when it spoke. Bubbles rose from the river near the troll's sunken mouth, though its lips barely moved.

"Where'd my little birds go?" asked a deep bass voice. "The birdsong is so soothing, so sleepy. . . ."

The troll started to drift off into a snore that sounded like the grinding of rocks. Emilie was forced to raise her voice to be heard over the din.

"I said, old troll, have you had any other visitors recently? Did any footsteps interrupt your dreams?"

"Footsteps?" said the voice. "Tiny feet that scamper and scurry and tickle me topsides and below. Yes. I remember footsteps. . . ."

Emilie gave Lukas a significant look—so someone had

been by recently. That was worrying. "Ask when they passed," he whispered. Better not to have too many people talking at once when you were trying to have a conversation with a sleepy stone troll.

"When, old troll?" said Emilie. "When did they cross?"

"Hmm? No, not long ago. Not long. Their tails tickle my undersides still. Hmm, heh, heh. Tickles."

Tails?

Lukas's hand went to his hatchet as understanding dawned on him. "Emilie! Get away from there!"

"Hmm?" rumbled the voice. "Such a racket."

Emilie waved Lukas angrily away and began whispering into the ear—a lullaby this time to help him to sleep once more. Soon he'd rest again, but there was no time for that now. Emilie didn't understand that they were all in danger, and not from the troll bridge.

Lukas grabbed Emilie around the middle and yanked her away, dragging her, protesting, toward the path, far faster than was safe. But somehow they managed to keep their footing and not spill off the side as they stumbled back to the others.

"What in heaven's name is the matter with you?" asked Emilie.

There wasn't time to explain. "Get everyone moving!" he called to Paul. "Make for the far bank! It's an ambush!"

Lukas's voice had the bark of an order about it, and Paul jumped to action.

Together they guided the other three along the bridge, over the shoulder and onto the outstretched arm toward the far bank. Lukas could see the shore just up ahead. They could've made a run for it, but Lukas didn't want to risk Carter falling behind.

Then, not twenty feet in front of them, shapes came scurrying up the sides. They'd been hiding underneath in the shadows, their tails tickling the very stone. The rats were waiting for them.

CHAPTER TWENTY-THREE

Max recognized the enormous leader rat at once. The patch of raw, puckered skin across its snout marked it as the same rat that had come for them in New Hamelin, the one Carter had burned with lamp oil. This time the creature was holding two knives, one in each hand, and with his thick, snakelike tail, he drew a third from his belt. Two more rats, one gray and one black, joined him while a smaller, fourth creature slinked some distance behind.

Max remembered Lukas boasting that he and Paul could take on two rats easily, but here were four. Still, the two boys wasted no time. Max heard Paul shouting in her ear to duck, and no sooner had she obeyed than an arrow sailed over her head. The black rat squealed as the arrow landed in its thick flank and it tumbled over the side, splashing into the river below.

It was the only free shot Paul was going to get, however, because the rats charged forward. They closed the distance so fast that Paul was forced to drop his bow and draw a long knife.

Max called to Carter as a rat made straight for them, snapping its jaws and hissing in anticipation. But Emilie got to Max's brother first, and though weaponless, she flung a small pouch in the air in front of the rat's face, and its contents exploded in a cloud of black powder. The rat reared backward, sneezing and pawing at its eyes. The air now smelled of pepper.

Emilie covered her own nose and mouth as she shooed Carter away from the coughing rat and behind his big sister. Emilie pointed to the spear in Max's hand, which Max had nearly forgotten about. "If you're planning on using that thing, now's the time!"

The rat, who had been momentarily blinded, recovered quickly. Its eyes, bloodshot and angry, glared at them. Without another warning, it lunged just as Max hefted her spear in front of her. The rat dodged Max's attack with ease, scampering back out of range, but it watched her now with a wary eye. Max placed herself between the rat and her brother.

She didn't dare look away from the creature, but in Max's periphery she could see that Paul and Lukas were busy with their own battle. They were trying to fend off the leader's three flashing knives. While the rest had come at them with teeth and claws, that one stood and fought like a human.

Max brought her attention back to her own opponent. "S-stay away," stammered Max as the rat advanced. "I don't want to hurt you; I'm . . . I'm a vegetarian!"

The rat cocked its head at her in confusion, then laughed. Or at least that was what it could've been—Max had never heard a rat laugh before. It was an ugly, unnatural sound. "King Marrow wants you alive," the rat rasped. "But I think I'll have a taste first!"

Then it ducked under Max's spear point faster than she would've thought possible. It came for her, its yellow teeth snapping, but just then the rat yelped in pain. It was Carter. He'd used his little knife to stab the rat's tail, and he was looking amazed that he'd done so.

The rat whipped its head around and clamped its powerful jaws around Carter's leg. Carter cried out as he was yanked to the ground. Max was too close to stab the creature, so she brought the butt of the spear down on the rat's head, instead. It squealed again, but it let go of Carter as it tried rising up on its hind legs to reach Max's throat. Just then the ground seemed to shift beneath their feet, and the rat lurched to one side and tumbled over. Max nearly fell, too, though she managed to keep her footing.

The rat scrambled back up to standing and opened its jaws for another attack, but this time Max didn't hesitate. This creature had gone after her brother.

The rat leaped forward, and Max stabbed with her spear. The point struck home, and the creature squealed and fell, rolling lifeless into the water below.

"Carter!" Max said, but Emilie was already by his side.

"I'm fine," he said. "Really."

Emilie lifted Carter's pants leg, which had been shredded by the rat's fangs. Max held her breath, afraid of what she would see.

"Well, look at that," breathed Emilie, relieved. The rat had bitten down on Carter's brace, and the sturdy plastic-and-steel contraption had protected him. The brace had a few teeth marks, but Carter was uninjured.

Emilie smiled at him as she helped him to his feet. "You wear your armor well, sir knight."

Max looked for Lukas and saw that the leader rat was gaining the better of the two boys. His whiplike tail caught Paul across the chest, and though the boy managed to avoid the blade, he was still knocked prone. The rat spared him little thought, however, as he threw his weight at Lukas and shoved the boy and his weapon aside.

"We need to move!" said Max.

"No, we have to help them!" said Carter, his little knife in his hand.

"You stay here—" Max began, but suddenly she was slipping again and had to throw her free hand out to keep from falling. The bridge was becoming unstable.

"It's the troll!" said Emilie. "I didn't have time to put him fully back to sleep."

Having broken past Lukas and Paul, the big rat turned his red eyes toward Carter. "To me, children," he rasped. "Come to Marrow!"

Then Max heard someone shouting her brother's name as Lukas returned to the fray. His sudden charge caught the rat called Marrow off guard, and the creature was forced to retreat a step to dodge the boy's wild hatchet swings.

"Get out of here, Carter!" Lukas shouted as he struggled to push the giant rat back.

"Wait!" said Carter. "I have an idea!" Carter turned

and ran back the way they'd come. It was a relief that Max's brother was running away. Maybe he could save himself, maybe follow the road back to New Hamelin. But she had to make sure the rats couldn't follow, so she joined Lukas, her spear at the ready.

Marrow stared down at the two of them, Lukas and Max side by side, and seemed to grin, though it was hard to discern any expression on his burned and ruined face. "Give me the boy, New Hameliner," he said. "Or you all die here."

Then Max's brother was yelling something, calling in the distance, and at first, she worried he might be in trouble. What if there were more rats back the way they'd come? But then she began to make out words.

"Hey!" her brother was shouting. "WAKE UP!"

He wasn't. He wouldn't . . .

Any more words died in the rumble of grinding rock and the roar of rushing water. Hundreds of nesting birds took flight as an earthquake shook the bridge beneath their feet and a tidal wave rushed up to swallow them all. The last thing Max saw was Marrow sliding toward the river, clawing desperately in vain to hold on to the bridge that was moving beneath him. And the last thing Max heard before tumbling headfirst into the waves herself was a deep, booming voice, the voice of a thoroughly annoyed giant troll, complaining about all the racket.

❧ CHAPTER TWENTY-FOUR ❧

Five children dragged themselves, sputtering and drenched, onto the far riverbank. As Max looked up at the enormous stone bridge that had, for lack of a better description, just rolled over onto its other side, she saw that the portion of the bridge that was now topside was green with algae and barnacles, and glittered wetly. There was less room for the river to flow freely since the bridge had shifted position, and the water spilled over the top in places, creating small waterfalls and white-water rapids. Downriver of the bridge, the deep Western Fork continued on its meandering path.

Max and her friends were half drowned but alive, although Lukas seemed especially shaken up by their dip in the river. And their weapons—her spear, Paul's bow and most of his arrows, Lukas's hatchet—were somewhere at the bottom of the Western Fork along with Lukas's and Paul's packs. Max had even been forced to kick off her boots so that they didn't drag her under, and so she was left standing on the pebbly shore wearing a single soggy sock.

She shivered as the breeze began to pick up. Was it Max's imagination or was today a little cooler than the day before? Maybe it was because she was drenched in river water. Either way, there were more pressing problems. On the other side of the river a pair of equally waterlogged shapes had pulled themselves out of the water and were slinking off into the forest, their long tails dragging behind them.

"It looks like two of them made it out," said Max. "The leader and that little one who didn't fight."

"The rats aren't known as great swimmers," said Paul. "They won't be following us." He glanced over at Max's brother. "Quite an idea he had."

"It was crazy, is what it was," said Max. "We're lucky we weren't drowned. Or crushed beneath the troll bridge."

"Still," said Paul. "It was something to see, wasn't it?"

Max turned her back on the scout and stomped over to where Lukas sat emptying sand out of his boots. The fight had frayed her nerves and the swim to shore had left her exhausted, but somehow she still had the energy to get mad.

"You promised me that Carter wouldn't get hurt," she said, jabbing a finger in the boy's chest.

"He didn't."

"He almost died! We all almost died! Fighting with giant rats might be everyday for you, but it's not for us."

Max could feel the stares of the others upon her, but she didn't care. Carter followed her and tried to calm her down with a hand on her arm, but she yanked it away. "If we keep this up, who knows how many of those rat things we'll run into—and now all of our weapons are at the bottom of the river!"

"Not all," said Carter, brandishing his little knife.

"Great," said Max. "I'll let you know if we need anyone to peel potatoes. You're going to get yourself killed!"

Carter tucked his knife away again, visibly stung. Then Max stormed off, yelping as she stubbed her bare toe on the rocky ground, which just made her all the madder.

They let her stew for a while, which was fine with Max. She sat alone on a driftwood log, her hands shoved in her damp pockets against the chill. When she finally heard footsteps approaching from behind, she turned and experienced a shock—Emilie was the last person she expected to see.

"Would you like some company?" asked Emilie.

No, Max wouldn't. People didn't storm off when they wanted company, but she didn't say that out loud. Instead, she shrugged and scooted over a few inches to make room on the log.

Emilie sat down next to her and began wringing river water out of her skirt. "I've sent the boys to fetch driftwood for a fire," she said. When Max gave her a look, she added, "Don't worry about Carter. Lukas won't let the boy out of his sight. But we could all use a good warming-up. And you and I could use a good talk."

Oh no. Was that to be Max's punishment? While the boys picked up sticks, she would have to sit here and be lectured by Emilie? Drowning might have been a better option.

"What do we have to talk about?" asked Max.

"Lukas has suggested that we turn south and make for the village of Shades Harbor. There we can resupply and regroup."

"A village sounds nice."

"Hmpf," said Emilie. "Wait until you see Shades Harbor. But nevertheless, it may be our only option. We cannot continue as we are. After that, we have to decide whether to press on or to turn back to New Hamelin. I think the choice is going to rest with you, in the end."

"And I know what you want," said Max. "You want us to go back."

"No," said Emilie.

Surprised, Max looked at the other girl. Emilie had fought their leaving in the first place, and Max had half suspected that she'd insisted on coming with them just so she could convince them to turn around. Max hadn't been expecting this change of opinion.

"I know," said Emilie. "That surprises you."

"Yeah," said Max. "It sure does."

Emilie wrung out more river water from her wet skirt, watching as it made a little stream in the pebbled sand beneath their feet. "You remember what you said to me, back at the village?"

Max shrugged. She'd said a lot of things to Emilie back at the village, and few of them nice.

"You said that I wear my pants," said Emilie.

"Um, it's 'wear *the* pants,' but like I said, that's only an expression. Actually, it's a stupid chauvinistic expression, but—"

"I understand what it means," said Emilie. "It means

leadership. But the thing about leadership is, it gets very lonely, and I don't make friends easily. It's not easy when you are Eldest Girl, but we are the only two girls on this journey with three thick-skulled boys, and though you and I might not be friends, it might make things simpler if we were at least . . . friendly."

"Oh," said Max. This was definitely not the conversation she'd expected. "Okay. Sure. I guess."

"Very good, that's settled, then," said Emilie, with the same matter-of-fact tone that one might use to agree on the price of eggs. "And since we are now being friendly, can I give you some friendly advice?"

"Okay," said Max warily.

"Don't give up on Carter."

"I'm not . . ."

"Back in the village you said that you didn't understand why girls shouldn't be allowed to put themselves in danger to help the ones they love."

"Well, I wasn't talking about—"

"I think the same should go for Carter," said Emilie. "What he did back at the bridge was foolhardy and reckless, but it was also just a little bit brilliant, wouldn't you say? And he might have saved our lives."

Max wasn't sure how to respond. Max had watched people coddle and patronize Carter his entire life, and she'd seen how hurtful it was—to be judged not capable without being given a chance. Most people thought they were being protective, but some were plain mean.

Just now, Max had been mean, and Carter deserved better from his sister, of all people.

"I'll apologize," said Max. "But I won't stop worrying about him."

"Nor should you," said Emilie, arching an eyebrow at Max. "I worry about those boys all the time! Dunderheaded bunch of know-nothings that they are."

Max and Emilie shared a smile. Then, having given up on ringing the water out of her sodden dress, Emilie stood up and sighed. "Now then," she said. "I'd better clear a place for the fire. Once we've dried off, we'll make for Shades Harbor. Maybe there I can find myself a pair of actual pants. This blasted skirt just won't do."

CHAPTER TWENTY-FIVE

The little dot labeled Shades Harbor on the Peddler's map turned out to be a small collection of buildings that could only be called a village if one were being generous. The harbor was arranged in a semicircle around a foggy little bay nestled in between two forested bluffs. A main street, its cobblestones wet from sea spray, wound past a number of oddly proportioned buildings. Some tilted precariously while others had been built in what could best be described as an upright zigzag shape. It wasn't a modern town, but its style, if there *was* one underneath all the bizarre architecture, reminded Carter of pictures of Victorian London. Gaslight lamps flickered in the fog, and in the distance Carter heard the clatter of a horse-drawn carriage echoing off the stone streets. Farther out into the bay, a lighthouse perched on an outcropping of stone.

Shades Harbor might have been called charming if it hadn't felt so lonesome.

Paul was wearing a sour face. "Now you see why I wanted to skip this place."

"The streets are empty," said Carter. Paul had told him that Shades Harbor was a village of ghosts, but though he could hear the distant sounds of activity, such as the clip-clopping of a horse and carriage and even a few voices, the town looked deserted.

"You'll see them soon enough," said Paul. "Though I wouldn't be calling those ghosts proper people."

"I'm sorry," said Max, interrupting their conversation. "What did you just say was down there?"

"Ghosts and dreamers," said Emilie. "It's said that Shades Harbor is where they land."

"It's true," said Paul. "Believe me, I've been there."

"Ghosts?" said Max. "You want us to go down into a town full of ghosts?"

"Nothing down there can hurt you," said Lukas. "They're harmless."

"Yeah, and what about the gray men?" asked Paul.

"Oh, not that again," said Lukas.

"What's he talking about?" asked Carter. "What are gray men?"

Lukas glared at Paul, but the other boy simply shrugged. "If you don't believe in them," said Paul, "then what's the hurt in telling?"

"I want to know," said Carter. Something unspoken was going on between Lukas and Paul, something Lukas obviously didn't want out in the open. They were behaving like grown-ups. "Can't be worse than the rats," added Carter.

"Fine," said Lukas. "You've heard that dreamers sometimes find their way to the Summer Isle, but the ones who do are only visiting, and they never stay long. Most don't even realize where they are—it's all just a part of the dream. Ghosts are more common, and they pass through this land, too, on their way to someplace else."

Carter nodded. He thought of the boy he'd seen chasing fireflies.

"Then there's the other kind of ghost," added Paul. "The not-so-friendly-like."

"No, there's *talk* of another kind," said Lukas, glaring again at Paul. "Of wraiths and revenants who refuse to pass on to the next world. Some call them gray men."

"Oh, if you're going to tell it, then tell it right!" said Paul, and he leaned close to Carter, lowering his voice. "See, the gray men won't move on because they have done something so wicked in their life that they're scared of the hereafter. They cling to the Summer Isle, and all that wickedness and fear eats away at them until they turn into something worse than ghosts. Ragged things they become, all dressed in tatters. And they haunt lonely, dark places, looking to share all that hurt. They've been here longer than anyone. They're ancient, and they're evil."

"Paul," warned Lukas. "It doesn't do any good to stoke the poor boy's fears."

Ghost stories were the only stories Carter didn't care for. Of course, Paul was not the most trustworthy kid Carter had ever met. How could he be sure the scout wasn't just trying to have some fun by scaring the littlest boy in the group? A *middle,* as he would be called.

Max must have been thinking the same thing. "Sounds like a boogeyman story," she said.

"It is," said Lukas. "Though Paul's version was a bit more colorful than I would have told it." Paul snorted, but Lukas ignored him. "The point is, in all our years here on the Summer Isle, I've never seen one. And neither has Paul."

"I haven't seen one with my eyes," said Paul. "But you spend enough time down there in Shades Harbor and you'll *feel* them watching you through those empty windows. Waiting for you to walk down the wrong alley. It's bad enough we'll have to pass by the Bonewood; can't see why we should risk the harbor, too."

"The Bonewood?" said Max. "That's a horrible name."

"That's the woods that grow around Shades Harbor," said Paul, pointing at the line of trees atop the nearby bluff. It was barely visible in the mist. "It's a mean place. You'll see for yourself. Another few miles and the Peddler's Road comes awfully close—"

"That's enough!" said Lukas, losing his patience. "We'll steer well clear of the Bonewood, but we are going down into the village. We're weaponless and out of food and water. I don't know about gray men, but if we run into any more rats in the condition we're in, we will be in trouble. That's certain."

"And you really think we can find supplies down there?" asked Carter. "In a village full of ghosts?"

"The residents can be traded with, after a fashion,"

said Emilie. "And Lukas is right—in all our years, no New Hameliner has ever seen a gray man."

"Not one that's lived to tell the tale," Paul muttered.

"I don't relish the idea of going down there, either," said Emilie. "But we won't survive on the road without supplies. We should be safe enough if we stick to the open places and stay together."

Carter looked down at the misty harbor village, at the lonely streets. Just for a moment, he thought he spotted a flash of movement, the yellow of a frilly dress passing between buildings. But it was gone as quickly as it appeared. A yellow dress, not gray rags.

A quick look to his sister confirmed that she had seen it, too, so it wasn't just Carter's imagination. It was also obvious from her expression that she was as freaked out about this place as he was. But Lukas was right when he said they couldn't keep on going empty-handed. Even if they turned back now, they would be forced to cross rat lands without any weapons to defend themselves.

What would an adventuring hero do? Of course, the hero would go down into the village. The hero wouldn't let simple ghost stories scare him away. But for the first time since coming to the Summer Isle, the name *hero* felt like it might be just another word. The rats were scary, but Paul's gray men story tapped into a deeper feeling. It was a fear born on those nights when he'd huddled under his covers in the dark, afraid to come out because he'd thought he heard something moving under the bed, because he'd spied a shadow that hadn't been there the moment before. Those fears had always been shapeless and indistinct, but thanks to Paul's story, they had form now. Carter's fears were gray like the grave, and covered in tatters.

Carter jumped as he felt Max's hand on his shoulder. "What do you think?" she asked. "We do need supplies."

"Oh, all right," answered Carter, summoning up a bravado that he didn't feel. He shook his head to clear the images of dead things in the dark. He didn't want to appear cowardly now. "Let's do it."

For once, Paul didn't take the lead. Instead, they followed Lukas off the Peddler's Road and down a little dirt path that wound between the two high bluffs. Shades Harbor was hidden between those forested hills and an ink-dark sea. Eventually, the dirt path gave way to a cobblestone street that snaked through the village. It looked to be the *only* main street in fact, with alleyways squeezing between the various oddly shaped buildings. Streetlamps were aglow with a weird bluish light, which did little to illuminate their way through the constant mist that rolled in off the water like waves. Down here in the village, the bright sun overhead was little more than a pale disk in the overcast sky, and now and then, voices came out of the fog—a fish seller calling, children laughing, a woman's voice rising in anger. They were the phantom sounds of a village full of people that weren't there.

Haunted was the only word for this place.

"You okay?" said Max, watching Carter.

"Yeah," said Carter. "Let's just keep moving."

The first building they passed was a lopsided shop with a sagging roof and a broken sign that dangled on its chain. If the shop had a name, the letters had long since faded. Carter used his sleeve to wipe the fog off the window before peering in. The darkened shop looked empty, but behind a long counter, he could see rows of rusty hooks hanging from the ceiling.

"I think it's an old butcher's shop," said Carter.

Lukas cleaned another patch of window and looked. "Yes. Could be knives in there, and no one to stop us from taking them." Lukas gave their companions a questioning look. No one spoke, but Paul emphatically shook his head *no*.

Carter agreed. Lukas swore the ghosts here couldn't hurt them, but even so, snooping around a haunted butcher's shop did not seem like a good idea.

"We'll keep it in mind," said Lukas after a moment. "In case we don't find anything more promising."

"Lukas, why are these shops here at all?" asked Carter. "I mean, if everyone's a ghost, who needs to go shopping?"

"It's hard to say," said Lukas. "But I think the shops are here because the ghosts expect them to be here, if that makes any sense. That's an empty butcher's shop, just waiting for a butcher to show up. Maybe he'll be a dreamer, or a ghost, but then he'll have his shop to haunt. I think the ghosts needed a village of their own—something familiar. Makes the journey easier, I guess."

Carter looked around them at the lonely streets, the empty windows and the drifting fog. He supposed that if ghosts were to dream up a village, Shades Harbor would be it.

With that, the five of them continued walking along the main village street. They passed several cottages and a few more empty businesses before the street brought them to the waterfront. Here the voices, snippets of conversations, grew louder, though they still came and went like the wind. Lukas stepped up to the dock and cupped his hands around his eyes as he stared out into the gloomy bay. He was searching for something.

"Paul, why can't we see them? The ghosts, I mean?" asked Max.

"That's because these ones know they're ghosts," said Paul. "And they're getting ready to move on. They don't care much what they look like anymore. When the ship comes in, you'll see them. The *fresh* ones."

"That's a terrible choice of words," said Max.

"Sorry," said Paul. "The recently deceased, then, for you who are easily offended. See, most of the newcomers don't know they're ghosts yet. They still look and talk like you and me. Only deader."

"We think that's why they come here," said Emilie. "They need time to realize what they are. Then they can move on."

"Not the gray men," said Paul.

"Enough about that," said Lukas. "You're scaring people."

"I'm not scared," said Carter, but his voice sounded fragile and small to his own ears. When his friends weren't watching the windows and the alleys, they were watching him, though they tried to hide it. This was ridiculous. Carter had faced down rat monsters, twice now, and won both times. But rats, even monstrous ones, could be fought. How did you fight a ghost?

"What about the dreamers?" Carter asked, trying to get his mind off ghosts for a while. "You mentioned dreamers, too."

"They end up here by accident, I think," said Lukas. "People get lost and wander out of their dreams for a while, I guess."

"How do you tell the difference between a ghost and a dreamer?" asked Max.

"One minute you'll be looking at a dreamer and the next he's gone," said Lukas. "The dreamer wakes up. But the ghosts take time to fade away. They don't leave until they're ready."

Carter remembered the boy chasing fireflies had disappeared like that. An eye blink and he was gone. The boy was a dreamer, then. For some reason, this made Carter feel better. He hadn't liked the idea of that happy little boy being anyone's ghost.

Max joined Lukas at the dock. "So are we just going to stare at the water all day?"

"I'm looking for the boat," said Lukas.

"What boat?" asked Max.

"That boat!" answered Lukas, clapping his hands together. "We're in luck."

Lukas's clapping echoed too loudly for Carter. The eerie silence of this place made him want to stay as quiet as possible. But there *was* a boat approaching. He could see it now, a large, glowing lantern swinging from the prow as the ship cut through the fog. It was an old-fashioned type of ship—a schooner, Carter thought it was called—with a black lacquered hull and full sails, though there was hardly any wind that Carter could feel. The long ship slowed to a stop as it lined up perfectly with the shore, and a gangplank extended off the deck and onto the dock below.

To Carter's relief, the ship was filled with people. Solid-looking people just as normal as he was—except for their clothing. A few were dressed in modern clothing—jeans and T-shirts—but the rest had stepped out of another century. Carter spotted a few women in long gowns, with twirling parasols, and there were men in top hats and coat tails. But the one thing they all had in common was a distinctive far-away expression, though not one of them seemed surprised to be here.

"Are they really . . . ," began Carter.

"Yep," whispered Paul. "What'd I tell you? Fresh ones. Don't even realize what's happened to them."

"But some of them are dressed like regular people and others look like they stepped out of another century. No offense."

Paul just shrugged. "I don't know. I guess I just assumed dead folk dressed oddly because they're, well, they're dead."

Carter wasn't so sure. The different styles might not bother Paul, but seeing the shades of people from different eras marching off that ship together made Carter wonder if there was even more to the Summer Isle than they thought. The New Hameliners didn't get older, but maybe time was more elastic than that. What if it was a place where ghosts and dreamers of every age could wander, because it was a place outside of time itself?

What then would that mean for the children of Hamelin who had disappeared over seven hundred years ago? And what would that mean for Carter's and Max's chances of ever getting home again?

"Hey, you all right?" asked Paul. "Something wrong?"

"What? No," said Carter quickly. "I, ah . . . I just expected them to be spookier, is all."

"You mean all rotten-like?"

"Maybe."

"I told you, these ones are fresh, so they don't get that they're dead. Their spirits look just the same as they do in everyday life. It's the ones that *know* they're dead that look awful. The ones that get angry about it."

"Those gray men?"

Paul nodded. "Best not talk about them here in town, though," he whispered. "Never know who's listening."

Carter glanced over his shoulder at the empty shops, the lonely alleyways. He didn't like the look of this place at all.

Most of the newcomers headed for the strange shops and homes of Shades Harbor while a few continued out of town. Carter heard someone sniffle behind him, and he turned to see Emilie wiping her nose on her sleeve. Were those tears in her eyes?

"Are you okay?" Carter asked her quietly. He didn't want to embarrass her in front of the others.

Emilie nodded. "None of them know," she explained. "All those people, and none of them have a clue as to what they really are. It strikes me as sad, is all. Silly of me."

Lukas seemed to be studying the faces in the crowd as they passed, as if looking for someone in particular, while Carter and the rest of his friends gave a man in a filthy, blood-stained apron a wide berth as he stalked off the gangplank.

The man was sweaty-faced and held a shiny meat cleaver in one hand. He stomped up the main street until he reached the butcher's shop with the faded sign. He paused there for a minute, then swung the door open and went inside.

"We are definitely not going in there now," said Max. Everyone, even Lukas, nodded in agreement.

"Ah, here we go," said Lukas. "This one looks promising. Come on!"

He'd started to follow a stout little man in suspenders and rolled-up shirtsleeves. The man was carrying two great big grocer's bags, and there was a pencil stuck behind his ear. He was mumbling to himself. "That's three pence for a dozen, should last us until Thursday. . . ."

"Come on," said Lukas. "Let's see where he goes."

Though Carter didn't know why they were doing so, they followed the little man to a storefront just down the street from the docks. This one was as lonely as the butcher's shop, with rows and rows of barren shelves. As they filed inside, the man slipped behind the counter. Then he looked up at Carter and his friends with an impatient smile, as if he'd been there all along.

"Well?" he said. "What can I get for you?"

"My friends and I are looking to outfit ourselves for a long journey," said Lukas.

"Yes, yes," said the man. "Well, as you can see, whatever you want, you'll find it here."

Carter and Max exchanged a look. The shop was empty except for the occasional cobweb. "I didn't know ghosts were also nuts," Max whispered, but not quietly enough, because the man shot her an annoyed look.

Lukas intervened. "Why don't you all wait outside? Emilie and I can take care of this." As the rest of them stepped outside, Carter glanced back into the shop. Emilie and Lukas were haggling with the man over the price of goods that weren't there.

"I know I shouldn't bother asking this," said Max, "but why are these people going about their business as if nothing's wrong? They just got off a boat in some weird little village, but no one's blinking an eye."

"Strange is normal when you're dead or dreaming, I guess," said Paul. "And people are creatures of habit, regardless. Either that fellow in there is a shopkeeper when he's awake or he *was* when he was alive. So he's a shopkeeper here."

"It's still weird," said Max.

"I didn't say I liked it," said Paul. "I'd just as soon be on our way. The living don't belong in Shades Harbor."

Carter agreed with Paul. He could feel it in the air, a cold prickle on the back of his neck. They weren't welcome here. Reflexively, he stepped aside as a man riding an old-style bicycle, with a front wheel larger than the back one, sailed past him and nearly ran over Paul. Paul let out a cry of surprise, though he suffered little more than a flutter of his hair blowing in the wind as the man pedaled by.

"Ghost wind," said Paul with a shiver.

Carter watched the man pedal away on his bicycle. He was yet another ghost out of time.

While they waited for Lukas and Emilie to finish bargaining for whatever it was they were bargaining for, the rest of them wandered back to the waterfront. The black ship was withdrawing its gangplank as it prepared to set sail.

"So it leaves empty like that?" asked Max.

"It's not empty," said Paul. "Listen."

Then Carter noticed it—the waterfront had grown silent. In the distance he could hear the sounds of the new arrivals as they opened doors and went about their business, but here near the water's edge, everything was quiet. The ghostly voices had all vanished.

"You mean there are ghosts on that ship?" asked Carter.

Paul nodded. "Those that were waiting on the docks when we arrived, the ones we heard but couldn't see. Those were the souls ready to move on. The black ships bring new shades to the harbor, and take away the ones that are sailing on to the next place. We may not be able to see them, but that doesn't mean they aren't on that ship. Just don't need bodies where they're going."

The ship raised its sails and disappeared into the fog.

Carter wondered what would happen if a living person tried leaving on that boat, and where it would take that person. He pulled his cloak tighter around him. Just the thought gave him the chills. Meanwhile, Max kept questioning Paul about the village, but Carter had heard enough. Careful not to wander far, he walked a few yards down the waterfront and gazed out at the sea. Were there other lands out there beyond the mists? Other places as wondrous and bizarre as the Summer Isle? Other harbors waiting for the black ships?

"You didn't come off the boat," said a voice, startling him.

Carter turned around to find a girl watching him. She didn't look like the others he'd seen. For starters, she appeared flimsy and flat, like she was the film projection of a girl rather than a real girl. She had her hair done up in fancy curls and wore an old-fashioned yellow dress edged with white lace—the same dress Carter had caught a glimpse of as they were coming into town.

"I saw some people coming down the road," she said, with an Irish lilt. "That was you, wasn't it?"

"Oh, yeah," said Carter, taken aback. "It was."

The girl nodded. "Thought so. My name's Isabelle. What's yours?"

"Carter." He wasn't sure if he should be standing there talking to a girl who might be a ghost, but he was afraid to turn his back on her. What did a ghost do to you if you were rude to it?

"How old are you?" Isabelle asked. "I'm turning ten next month."

"I'm already ten," said Carter.

"Fibber," said the girl. "You're not older than me; you're not tall enough."

"I am, really," said Carter. "I'm ten."

Isabelle crossed her arms over her chest and sized Carter up. "Maybe," she said. "But you don't look it. You're sort of squat."

"I haven't hit my growth spurt, is all," said Carter.

"Is that why your leg's like that?" she asked.

"No," said Carter. He was no longer scared of the girl, but he was getting slightly annoyed. "My leg has nothing to do with it."

As Carter watched Isabelle move, he noticed that the sea mist wasn't blowing past her; it was blowing through her, even as it was getting thicker here on the waterfront. He remembered what Paul had said about the dead slowly fading away as they realized what they were. This girl was definitely a ghost, then. He suddenly felt sorry for her, and that fact alone made Carter want to give her the benefit of the doubt.

"How long have you been here?" he asked.

"Hmm. Came in on another boat, whenever that was," she said. "I got sick, back at our house, then I woke up on the boat and I was all better. Lots of us then, not so many now. Haven't been able to find my parents, but I've made a friend. The professor's been teaching me letters."

"The professor?"

Isabelle nodded. "He says he can show me how to read. Mother will be so proud."

This professor must've been another ghost, like Isabelle. Carter turned to call to his sister but suddenly realized that the fog had grown so dense that he could no longer see where she was. He could hear the lapping of the waves nearby, but the sea itself was hidden in the thick mist.

Carter called his sister's name, then Paul's. After a moment, he could hear Max calling back, but she sounded a long way away. And he couldn't even tell which direction he was facing.

"Who are you calling for?" asked Isabelle.

"Uh, my friends," said Carter. He took a deep breath, trying not to panic. Slowly he turned around in a circle, peering this way and that, but all he could see was more fog. "I think . . . I think I'm a little lost."

"Well, if you're lost, I can take you to the professor," said Isabelle. "He's ever so smart, and I'm sure he can help you find your friends."

"Uh . . ." He could hear Max calling his name again, only it sounded even farther away this time.

"I'm here!" he shouted. His voice came echoing back to him, but this time there was no other reply.

"It's just over there," said Isabelle, pointing to something in the mist Carter couldn't see. She reached out her hand to take Carter by the arm, but her incorporeal fingers found no purchase. They were just a cold tickle along Carter's skin.

"Now, that's odd," Isabelle said, genuinely surprised. "I can't touch you." But she didn't dwell on it. The ghost girl turned and began drifting away into the mist. "Follow me."

Carter didn't know what to do. He didn't want to follow her, but if he didn't, he would be left here all alone. Max had disappeared, and Carter was lost in this unnatural fog. He was afraid of setting off blindly on his own for fear of stumbling into the sea.

"Come on, Carter," Isabelle called again. "I'll take you to him!"

Carter felt himself beginning to hyperventilate, and he bit down on his cheek so hard that he tasted blood. Another moment of indecision and Isabelle would be gone as well, and Carter would be truly alone.

"Wait up!" he called.

Isabelle waited for him, and when he caught up with her, she turned and pointed. "You see? It's just over there, not far at all."

Isabelle had led him away from the waterfront, and the mist farther inland was not quite as thick as it had been closer to the shore. Here it was thin enough that he could make out a cottage sitting at the entrance of a narrow alley. Unlike the rest of the buildings, this little house didn't look dingy at all. In fact, it actually looked lived-in. The windows were lit with a pleasant warm glow that chased away some of the gloom.

"The professor's ever so smart," said Isabelle. "Come on."

The cottage was surrounded by a low, wrought-iron gate, which Isabelle glided through without seeming to notice. Carter was forced to unlatch the gate and he winced as it creaked with years of disuse. No one had passed through that gate in a long time. No one living, anyway.

The thought gave Carter pause, and he stopped where he was, still a few yards from the door. Then, out of the corner of his eye, he saw something move in the alley next door. When he tried peering that way, all he saw was mist and shadows, but he thought he could hear movement as well. It sounded like cloth dragging along stone. Carter suddenly pictured gray skin wrapped in tattered rags, and long fingers reaching out through the fog. . . .

Isabelle noticed his hesitation. "You coming?" she said.

Carter opened his mouth, but he couldn't speak. He couldn't take his eyes off that alley. Was that a shape he saw forming there?

"Fine," said Isabelle. "I'll just pop in and fetch him, then. You stay right where you are. Don't go anywhere."

Isabelle disappeared through the door as easily as light passing through a window. Carter backed away from the alley. He wanted to run, but he didn't dare turn his back on the thing in the alley. The shape was drawing closer.

Just then the cottage door swung open and light spilled forth. Isabelle reappeared next to a tall, thin man wearing a pair of bent glasses that were instantly, achingly familiar. The man was puffing on a tobacco pipe as he ran his fingers through his hair, trying to smooth his ever-present cowlick—the same cowlick Carter had inherited from him.

There was a final rustle of movement from the alley as the shadow, or whatever it was, fled. But Carter barely noticed, as his full attention was now on the figure in the doorway.

"There he is, Professor," said Isabelle, pointing to Carter and smiling. "That's my very newest friend."

Carter's father, standing next to her, blinked in surprise. "Carter? What on earth are you doing here?"

CHAPTER TWENTY-SIX

Max had been chatting with Paul when she realized she'd lost track of time, and of Carter. A dense fog had rolled in all of a sudden, and she couldn't see five feet in front of her. Max and Paul walked along the waterfront, calling her brother's name. She could hear him calling in return, but it was hard to find him. Max was starting to worry, but the mist quickly rolled back out to sea, and when it did, they found Carter sitting on the ground outside a nearby cottage. He had his knees drawn up tight against chest, and his cheeks were flushed from crying. Lukas and Emilie appeared at the opposite end of the street with bundles in their arms, but Max was more concerned for her brother.

"Carter," Max said, hurrying toward him. "Hey, what's wrong?"

Carter sniffed and looked up at his sister with bloodshot eyes. "I saw Dad," he said.

"What? What do you mean?"

Carter glanced back at the little cottage. "He was in there. I talked to him, Max. It was Dad."

Max felt the others walking up behind her, but she didn't turn around.

"In there?" she asked. Carter nodded. How could their father be in this place, in a town full of ghosts? Unless . . . no, her brother was mistaken. He had to have been.

"Paul, stay with Carter for a minute."

Paul gave her a worried look. "Maybe you shouldn't."

"Just stay with him."

The cottage door was slightly ajar, but not enough that she could see inside. For a moment, she considered knocking but then chided herself for being ridiculous. She grabbed hold of the door handle—it was cold to the touch. Then she took a breath to steel herself and gave the door a push.

It was a sparse, one-room cottage. Dust motes floated through the air and were sent swirling as she swung the door open wide. A small table and two chairs sat in the center of the room. A wooden bed with no mattress was pushed up against one of the walls next to a cold fireplace. A thick coat of dust covered the floor, and Max wondered idly if ghosts left footprints.

She was just turning around to tell her brother that the cottage was empty when she caught a whiff of something that made her gasp aloud. The smell of apple-y tobacco smoke lingered in the air. Her father's pipe.

"He was here," Carter said, standing in the doorway. "There was a fire going in the fireplace, and lamps lit and everything. A girl named Isabelle brought me here, but I don't know where she went."

"And you saw him?"

Carter nodded.

"What did he say?"

"He was surprised to see me, but he seemed glad. He was confused. He wasn't sure where he was or how he'd gotten here, but he was passing the time by teaching Isabelle to read. He asked about you, Max. He wanted to know if you were all right."

Hearing that made Max's chest tighten. She was trying to keep herself together, for Carter's sake.

"He say anything else?"

"I told him we were trying to get home, and he said he'd like that. He said he missed us and he loved us."

Carter was crying again, and Max felt her own resolve giving way.

"But, Max," said Carter, through his tears. "I don't know if he was dreaming or if . . . if . . ."

Her brother couldn't finish the sentence, but he didn't have to. What he'd wanted to say was that they didn't know if their father had been a dreamer . . . or a ghost.

Max fought against the tears. If she let herself go, she might crumple beneath the weight of it all, and that wouldn't help her brother. It wouldn't help anyone. She took her brother by the shoulder and backed him away from the cottage.

"Could it be true?" she asked the others. "Could it really have been our dad?"

Emilie and Lukas exchanged looks. Then Emilie said, "I know what you are thinking, but Carter said your father disappeared in front of his eyes, yes?"

"Yeah," answered Carter. "We were talking, and then he just suddenly vanished. Like the boy I saw back in the Shimmering Forest."

"He was a dreamer, then," said Emilie, nodding matter-of-factly. "Dreamed himself here, and then he woke up. Remember what Paul said—ghosts are slow to fade."

Max felt her brother's fingers close around hers. "So that wasn't Dad's ghost?" he asked. Emilie smoothed Carter's hair back from his forehead. It was such a simple gesture, yet it was filled with love and reassurance. It was exactly the kind of thing that Carter needed right now from his big sister, and yet all Max could do was stand there. She was holding herself together with fraying thread.

"Your father is safe, and I think maybe he's looking for you, Carter, in his own way," said Emilie. "In his dreams."

Then it struck her, just how thick she had been all this time. Of course Emilie understood what Carter was going through and what Max was going through—every New Hameliner did. Max had been acting as if Carter and she were special. She'd demanded things of these other children—she'd threatened and cried and felt sorry for herself and worried for her brother. While every adult these New Hameliners had ever known had long since turned to dust. Yet these children hoped. They hoped that there was magic enough out there to return them not just to *where* they came from, but also to *when* they came from. It seemed a feeble hope to Max, yet the New Hameliners clung to it with everything they had.

From this moment forward, Max would need to follow their example if she was going to get her brother home. If anyone hoped to escape this land of eternal childhood, then they were all going to have to grow up a little.

Max put an arm around her brother and gave him a kiss on the forehead. "Emilie is right, Carter. Dad's alive and well, I know he is."

"How?" asked her brother.

"Because, for once, let's believe in happy endings. What do you say?"

CHAPTER TWENTY-SEVEN

Despite their deep misgivings, they agreed to spend the night in Shades Harbor. Evening was upon them, and according to the map, the next several miles of road skirted the edges of the Bonewood. Even Paul had to admit that a room in the village was probably safer than making camp anywhere near that notorious forest. After a little searching, they found a small inn run by a plump woman who seemed to be dreaming that she was the concierge at a luxury hotel.

While the rooms were dusty and smelled of mildew, Carter welcomed the chance to sleep in a bed again. And once Lukas got a fire going in the fireplace, the room almost started to feel cozy, or as cozy as it could get in a village full of spirits.

"Well, here's what we've managed to get," said Lukas as he unrolled a large bundle onto one of the beds. Inside was an assortment of food and supplies. There were a few wedges of cheese, some trail rations made up mostly of nuts and dried fruit, a few changes of clothing, though no pants for Emilie and no shoes to replace Max's lost boots. But there were weapons—three long daggers, each easily the length of Carter's forearm.

"No bows?" asked Paul, frowning.

"We were lucky to get these," said Lukas, and he handed one to Paul and another to Max. The third he stashed in his own belt.

"But how did you get them at all?" asked Max. She was weighing the blade in her hand, as if she knew what she was looking for. "I still don't understand it. The shops here are all empty, so how did you find weapons and food?"

"There's a trick to dealing with these ghosts and dreamers," said Lukas. "To them, this whole place is just a part of their dream, or the life they think they are still living. Think about it—they aren't wearing real clothes, and yet not a one of them is naked. If they believe they are wearing clothes, then they are wearing clothes. That butcher we saw getting off the boat believed he was still a butcher, so he carried the tools of his trade."

"A bloody, disgusting-looking meat cleaver," said Paul.

"Yes," said Lukas. "So we just had to convince the shopkeeper that he was selling what we needed."

"Wait," said Carter. "So if you ask one of these people for anything, it will magically appear?"

"It didn't turn out to be that simple," said Emilie. "These ghosts and dreamers can be stubborn, and that shopkeeper loves to haggle. I was forced to trade away most of my herbs and my tea kettle."

"But if all this stuff was dreamed up, won't it just fade away again?" asked Carter.

Lukas kicked one of the bedposts. "This whole town was dreamed up by someone a long time ago, and it's still here."

"What he's saying is, he doesn't know," added Paul. "Might last, might not. Either way, better dig in while you can." With that, the boy plopped down in front of the fire and started gnawing a hunk of cheese. Emilie joined Paul next to the warm rug, and the scout broke off a hunk of cheese and shared it with her without comment. Carter thought about joining them, but something about the way they were sitting together felt too private to disturb. Maybe they were finally coming to some kind of truce, and Carter didn't want to risk messing that up.

"We should still have several weeks of good hot weather ahead of us," said Lukas, pointing out at the evening sky, which was turning the color of wine as the sun sank low. "Isn't that so, Paul?"

"I suppose," said Paul, spitting bits of cheese rind into the fire. "If that map of yours is right, then I'd say we'll cross the Eastern Fork in a day or two. After that, we turn north and make for the tower. I give us a fortnight's travel yet, at the pace we're keeping."

At the pace we're keeping. Though he didn't come out and say it, Carter understood what Paul had meant. They'd be going faster if they didn't have to slow down for Carter.

"The road grows more dangerous from here on out," said Paul. "Even if the rats are behind us, there's the Bone-wood ahead of us. And beyond the Eastern Fork is the Deep Forest, and elves. We won't find any hospitality there."

"Then we'll keep on going," said Lukas. "The Peddler's Road will let us bypass the Deep Forest entirely, so elves shouldn't be a problem."

As this seemed to be the final word on the subject, Carter tried to find something to do. This was, he realized, the first time he'd actually been bored since coming to the Summer Isle. He spent a few minutes absentmindedly pulling bits of stuffing from one of the mattresses and tossing them into the fire. He had to stop, though, because the room was beginning to smell like burnt hair. Max gazed out the window, and Paul was snoring softly in front of the fire. His head had fallen onto Emilie's lap, and though she was staring at it as if a spider had just crawled onto her, she had yet to smack his forehead to wake him up.

Lukas laid the Peddler's map across one of the beds and studied it. When he noticed Carter watching him, Lukas grinned. "I keep checking it to see if anything's changed. But it's the same as the day you two arrived. The Peddler had always claimed that this map was enchanted, but before the Black Tower appeared, nothing unusual ever happened."

Carter joined Lukas on the bed. He let his eyes follow the dotted-line road from New Hamelin past the Western Fork and all the way to Shades Harbor. It seemed strange that despite the days of travel and everything they'd been through, they hadn't explored more than a few inches of that map. There, to the right of Shades Harbor, the Bonewood was clearly marked; it lay between them and the Eastern Fork. It wasn't a big forest, certainly not as big as the Shimmering Forest or the Deep Forest, to the southeast. Carter almost asked why it was named the Bonewood, but then he decided he didn't really want to know. Not right before bedtime, in any case.

"Lukas," said Carter. "What do you think we'll find there at the Black Tower?"

Lukas rubbed his chin as he considered his answer. From her spot on the floor, Emilie turned to look, and Max watched from the window, curious, too. They were wondering the same thing.

"All we have to go on is the map and the prophecy," said Lukas at last. "*Only when the last son of Hamelin appears and the Black Tower found will the Piper's prison open and the children return safe and sound.* Not many details to go on, huh?"

"No," said Carter. "Not really."

"Well," said Lukas. "If we believe the prophecy is talking about you, which I do, then maybe there's some kind of doorway there, or a portal that only you can open. Or find. I don't know. But when the Piper brought us here, we passed through a cave in a mountain, I remember that much. And he brought you two here, so there have to be ways to go between home and the Summer Isle."

Carter remembered all those stories his dad had collected and how there seemed always to be a twist. It used to drive Carter crazy when he was little—the terrifying beast was really a cursed prince; Anansi the trickster was really at home in the briar patch, and didn't fear the briars at all. Carter wondered if their own adventure, their story, wasn't yet due for another twist.

"What is the Black Tower?" said Carter. "The prophecy says that the Piper's prison will be opened."

"Yes," said Lukas. "That part worries me, too."

"Maybe the tower is his prison," said Carter. "Maybe the Piper has to take us home."

Lukas's expression grew hard as he slowly rolled up the Peddler's map. "If so, it's the least he owes us."

Carter had never seen such a grim look on Lukas's face before, but he understood it. The Piper had stolen them all away from their homes and their families and abandoned them here to fend for themselves against monsters. Like Lukas, Carter wasn't sure how he'd react if he saw the Piper again.

The talking quieted down again after that, and nothing interrupted the crackle of the fire. Each child seemed lost in his or her thoughts, or maybe they were just enjoying the quiet and each other's company. A warm fire, soft beds and a roof over their heads. Who knew when they'd feel this kind of comfort again?

"The rest of us should get some sleep," said Emilie after a while. She nudged Paul awake, and he looked a little terrified when he realized where he'd been sleeping. But Emilie didn't comment on it. "We have a long walk ahead of us," she said.

As they divided up the beds, Carter caught his sister watching him. He knew she worried about him, and Carter wished he could do something to reassure her that he would be okay. He had Lukas, Emilie, Paul and, most important, his big sister to look out for him. Carter would be fine.

Someone suggested that even though they were sleeping indoors, it might be a good idea to set a watch. This time they split the duty between the five of them, instead of making Lukas and Paul shoulder all the responsibility. Lukas balked at first, but Paul gladly accepted the chance to get a little extra sleep.

It was late when Paul woke Carter to take his shift at watch, though the sky outside was still only a sunset purple. Paul told Carter that he'd nearly woken him earlier, because the boy had been mumbling in his sleep and looked as if he was having a bad dream. But all Carter could remember of the dream was music. Paul gave Carter a blanket to wrap himself in as he sat by the window and then took Carter's place in the bed next to Lukas. The scout was snoring in minutes.

No one woke Lukas for the next shift, and it wasn't until sunrise that anyone noticed that Carter was gone.

CHAPTER TWENTY-EIGHT

When they were little, Max and Carter used to play hide-and-seek in the hallways of their old apartment building. It was never much of a challenge for Max, as Carter wasn't very good at the game, and there were only so many places you could hide in a long hallway. But Carter had still been young enough to think that if he couldn't see someone, there was no way that person could see him. So his favorite hiding spots tended to be even more obvious than the stairwell and the laundry room. He liked to hide in one end of the hall with his eyes shut, or the other end of the hall with his eyes shut. Max's job, even then, had basically been to wander up and down the hall and pretend not to see him.

Until one day, when Max finished counting to twenty and opened her eyes and her brother was gone. It was impressive at first, not seeing him in his usual places. She checked the laundry room and the stairwell, but he wasn't there. Max checked back inside their apartment in case he'd somehow gotten in without her noticing.

In those next few minutes, Max felt a new kind of fear— a growing dread that her brother might really be gone. Time began to slow down, dreamlike, but she wasn't asleep. And still Carter didn't answer her calls. In a real panic, she ran inside and found her mother, and though barely intelligible because of her crying, she confessed that she'd lost her little brother.

It didn't take more than five minutes for her mother to find him. Carter, it turned out, had knocked on the door of his best friend down the hall, something he'd never thought of doing before, and when their mom found him, he was sitting on the neighbors' sofa, watching cartoons with his friend. He'd been very pleased with himself until he saw his sister's face.

After that day, Max never played hide-and-seek with her brother again.

Max's heart fluttered inside her chest like a bird in a shaking cage. It didn't help that she was running barefoot, but she didn't have time to stop and examine her sore feet. Carter was out there somewhere, alone.

How long had they been running? An hour? Two? Long enough that she'd barely registered the change in the land-scape. How the road turned northward and how the Bone-wood seemed to chase it until the borders of that fearful forest butted up against the road itself. There were places where the pale trees had grown close enough to touch.

All Max knew was that she had to struggle just to keep up. Even Emilie was ahead of her, though not by much. She could barely see Paul's shape in the distance as he followed Carter's tracks in the road. They'd wasted time scouring the village for him until Paul had spotted a new set of tracks leading out of Shades Harbor and east along the Peddler's Road; luckily for them, Carter's limp made his footprints distinctive.

Max's tongue was covered with a film of grit, and her mouth tasted of metal. Each gasp hurt, and she clutched at a stitch in her side until it felt like her innards would burst. Lukas judged that since her brother hadn't woken him up for his shift, Carter had somewhere between a three- and five-hour head start. The good news was that it wasn't so much time they couldn't make it up if they ran hard. The bad news was that Carter was all alone.

Max had no physical reserves of strength left to call on, so she relied on her anger to keep her going. Anger at her brother for leaving her and anger at herself for losing him. At every bend in the road, she half expected to find him sitting on the ground and laughing at her. But she knew deep in her gut that this was no joke. Carter would have never run off in the middle of the night. Something had taken him. It didn't matter if they were only following one set of tracks—Carter had been kidnapped.

She was so tired, she barely saw the ground in front of her and almost ran over Lukas as he came to a stop. Up ahead, Paul was now walking in a circle as he studied the road. Max looked questioningly at Lukas—there was no chance her parched throat could make words.

"We have to rest," said Lukas, breathing hard. "For a moment, at least."

Max tried to shout *Why?* at Lukas, but all that came out was a painful cough. Someone was handing her a flask of water. She took it without thanks and wet her throat.

"What . . . ," she tried again. Her voice was still raw and dusty, but at least it was working. "What do you mean? Why are we stopping? Have you found something?" Words came out in a tumble.

No one would look her in the eye. At first she thought it was because they were all ashamed that they wanted to stop and rest, but then Max realized they were not avoiding her eyes; they were staring at her feet. Her feet were bloody and torn. It was funny—she'd known they hurt, but now that she saw the condition they were in, it felt like she was standing on a bed of coals.

"I'm fine," she said through gritted teeth.

"Sit down," ordered Emilie. "We need to clean and bandage those feet."

"I can walk!"

"Eh, sorry," said Paul. "Leaving a blood trail, even on the Peddler's Road, is a very bad idea. There're things out there we don't want following us."

Things out there . . . And her brother. Her little brother, alone. When Max found Carter, she was going to kill him.

"Paul and I will scout ahead while you get fixed up," said Lukas, placing a hand on Max's shoulder. "We don't need to rest."

"We don't?" whined Paul, but Lukas ignored him.

"If we keep up our pace, I'm sure we'll find Carter before too long," said Lukas. "We have to be close."

It was foolish for Max to protest. The truth was, these New Hameliners were in much better shape than she was, and she would probably slow them down even without her wounded feet. Their best chance of finding her brother now was speed. Reluctantly, Max nodded and allowed Emilie to help her sit on the side of the road.

"You be careful," said Emilie to Lukas.

"Don't worry," answered Paul. "*We* will."

"You be careful, too," said Lukas. "Both of you. We'll be back soon. Hopefully with Carter."

Then Paul and Lukas were off. Exhaustion was catching up with them now, too. They moved at a jog rather than a sprint. Nevertheless, within minutes the pair of them were out of sight.

Emilie took a swig from her flask, then handed it over to Max. "Don't drink too fast or you'll cramp."

Max forced herself to sip rather than gulp. She was far from full, but she heeded Emilie's advice and gave the flask back to her. Emilie used it to wet a cloth from her pouch and began to dab at Max's feet. They barely resembled feet anymore, just two swollen lumps of cuts and bruises. Max winced as Emilie cleaned what dirt she could out of the wounds.

"I have some ointments that I kept," said Emilie. "They should help, but they sting."

"I can handle it."

The girl looked up at Max. "They sting a lot."

Emilie was right about the stinging, and Max gave a sharp gasp as Emilie rubbed a green paste into her wounds. It might as well have been salt.

"So, back where you come from," said Emilie, "did you have someone special?"

Max gritted her teeth against the pain and stared at Emilie, incredulous. Was this really the time for girl talk? But then she realized that Emilie was probably just trying to get Max's mind off her feet, and off of Carter.

"If you mean do I have a boyfriend, no," said Max. "Ouch, ouch! I'm going to need that foot, you know?"

Emilie ignored her complaining. "Was there ever anyone special?"

"I'm not even thirteen yet."

Emilie shrugged. "I was just curious." Then she began to wrap Max's foot in a strip of cloth, which hurt a lot less than the ointment. Max watched Emilie work for a minute before something occurred to her.

"Why do you have boyfriends on the brain?"

Emilie blushed. "I do not have . . . whatever it is you just said. I was only being friendly."

Then Max remembered last night in the little inn and a certain boy Emilie had sat next to the entire evening. Even when he'd fallen asleep and started to drool in her lap.

"Wow," said Max. "I wouldn't have seen that coming. Maybe you and Lukas, but Paul? Never."

Emilie poured water on a new cloth and began dabbing at Max's other foot, less gently this time. "I'm sure I don't know what you are talking about," said Emilie.

"It's okay," said Max. "I'd bet he likes you, too."

As if she couldn't stop herself, Emilie blurted out, "Do you think so?"

"Why do you think he spends all his time trying to bug you? Boys are weird like that, but it's a pretty good sign, I'd guess."

Emilie went back to cleaning Max's foot. "He really is insufferable. Not enough sense between his ears to fill a thimble."

"I know. But I don't think our brains get to choose these things."

"Pish," said Emilie. "I'm sure it'll pass. Like indigestion or a sour stomach, I will just have to wait it out until it goes away." She finished cleaning the other foot and reached for the ointment. "Now, you might want to bite down on something. This next part's going to hurt again."

After Max's feet were cleaned and cared for, Emilie used strips of her own skirt to make wraps, and she bound Max's feet as best she could. The rags would have to serve as makeshift shoes for the time being.

With nothing left to do, the waiting soon became unbearable. Max had just insisted that the two of them start to follow when Lukas appeared on the road up ahead. His face was ashen, and not from running.

"What?" asked Max, her heart in her throat. "What's wrong?"

"It's your brother's tracks," he said, shaking his head. "Carter's left the road. He's gone into the Bonewood."

❧ CHAPTER TWENTY-NINE ❧

It was becoming Carter's habit to wake up in strange places. This time, the last thing he remembered was sitting watch in their room back in Shades Harbor. He'd been fighting to stay awake and so moved his stool closer to the window, where he could feel the sea breeze against his cheeks and smell the salt in the air. Away in the distance, someone was playing a pipe. It was a lovely tune. . . .

Then he'd woken up here, wherever *here* was. Carter was lying on a hard bench in a cluttered room with two barred windows on either side. There was a long, solid-looking table beneath one window, covered in jars and strange instruments. He saw a mortar and pestle, a little oil burner and a butcher's block with an ominous dark stain in the middle. One corner held a lumpy bed, and another a rocking chair. In the center of the room was a bubbling cauldron and a cast-iron stove.

The floor was covered with what Carter had assumed at first to be a bearskin rug, but upon further examination, it was clear that this rug had never been a bear. Whatever creature that pelt had belonged to had been very big, and disturbingly human-shaped.

"Ogre skin," said a little voice. Carter whipped around to see a little creature, perhaps a foot tall, in a cage dangling on a chain. He was furry, and at once reminded Carter of Tussleroot the kobold, only this one was not nearly as potato-shaped. "The rug is mostly ogre, I think."

"Who are you?" asked Carter. "Where am I?"

"My name's Bandybulb," said the creature. "And you are in Grannie Yaga's hut. Sorry to say."

Carter glanced at the disgusting skin rug, then at the butcher block and over to the oven. Nothing reassuring about any of that.

"I don't know who Grannie Yaga is, but I think I'd better get going," said Carter, and he made for the door. Thankfully the handle turned—it was unlocked—and he cautiously pulled it open just a crack, barely enough to peek outside. He was inside a hut built in a clearing surrounded by a forest of ugly yellowish-white trees. Carter nearly yelped when a wind chime made from skulls began to rattle above his head, but there didn't seem to be anyone out there to hear it. At least, no one he could see.

Carter wasn't fast, but he decided it was time to make a run for it, anyway.

"Wait!" called Bandybulb from his little cage. "Take me with you! Please don't leave me with her."

Carter paused, frozen between the instinct to flee for his life and the desire to help someone in need.

Shutting the door softly, he turned and quickly made his way to Bandybulb's cage. There was an obvious door mechanism, but he couldn't find a latch to open it.

"Thank you, thank you," said Bandybulb as Carter fiddled with the cage door. "Grannie Yaga keeps me around because she says Bandybulb makes her laugh, but she has fearful eating habits."

Carter was still struggling with the little cage when the hut's front door swung open. "Too late," cried Bandybulb as he slumped back down in his cage.

In hobbled a hunchbacked old crone with a nose so long and so crooked that it dipped past her chin. She leaned on a cane as thick as a cudgel and carried a lumpy sack slung over one shoulder. She didn't look particularly strong or dangerous, but Carter had read enough stories to know better. You could never underestimate the witch in the woods.

For a second, Carter looked past the old woman and into the woods outside the door. He probably wouldn't have made it anyway, he thought. He doubted he was fast enough to outrun even an old woman.

The old woman, who had to be Grannie Yaga, smiled a toothless smile at Carter and slammed the door shut behind her.

"Ehhh," she mumbled as she pulled out a long key from her apron and locked the door with a heartbreaking click.

Carter's hand drifted to his belt. He still had his knife there, at least.

Then Grannie Yaga tossed her sack onto the table and crossed the room to her rocking chair. Carter noticed for the first time that there were two pairs of fake teeth, like dentures, hanging from pegs next to the chair. One set looked made of wood. The other, rusty iron.

Carter felt Bandybulb tense up as the little creature pressed his face to the bars of his cage and whispered, "You better hope she chooses the wooden ones!"

Grannie Yaga paused in front of the teeth and glanced back over her shoulder at Carter. She chuckled as he took an involuntary step away, backing himself right into the wall. The windows were barred, and the door was locked. There was nowhere else to go. Carter was as trapped as Bandybulb in his cage. He gripped the hilt of his knife, hard.

Then Grannie Yaga reached up and snatched the wooden teeth off their hook. There was a disgusting sucking sound as she fitted the awkward artificial teeth into her mouth.

"Now, that's better," she said, turning back around. "You can let go of that knife for now, sweet boy. These wooden ones is for talking. The *wooden* ones is, anyways."

Grannie Yaga plopped down heavily in her rocking chair and smiled. Somehow Carter found the courage to speak. "How did I get here?"

"Ooh, are we playing questions and answers, then?" said Grannie Yaga. "Fine. You asked first, so Grannie will answer first. You was found sleepwalking in the woods, and I brought you here safe and sound before any ogres could step on you. Now's my turn. What's your name, sweet boy?"

"Carter Weber," answered Carter.

"That so?" said Grannie Yaga. "You sure? Doesn't smell like your name."

"I'm sure," said Carter. It only just occurred to him that maybe he should have lied about his name, but it was too late now, anyhow. "Is it my turn to ask a question?"

She nodded.

"Are you going to eat me?" He figured he might as well get to the point.

Grannie Yaga broke out into a hideous cackle. It sounded like someone shaking a string of tin cans. Bandybulb covered his little ears and hid his head. "I ain't done it yet," she said. "Could have made sweet meat pie from my sweet, sweet boy or stolen the breath out a your body and jarred it up tight like jam. Still might, if you don't watch your manners. But as you see, my oven's cold yet, and Grannie's good teeth are hung on the wall."

She patted the cast-iron stove behind her, and Carter was relieved to see that it wasn't lit. The cauldron, on the other hand, did have a small flame beneath it, and he could see the occasional frothy bubble rise up from the top of whatever foul brew she was cooking in there. Luckily, it was a small cauldron and there was no way Carter could have fit inside it. Not whole, anyway.

"So you be polite and proper and Grannie won't need her good teeth," said Grannie Yaga, gesturing to the rusty iron pair hanging behind her. "But now's my question. Where's your sister?"

"What?" said Carter before he could stop himself. "How did you know I have a sister?"

"Ah, ah," said Grannie Yaga. "My question still. Your answer."

"Fine," said Carter. Maybe it was for the best that he hadn't lied about his name. Grannie Yaga seemed to know more about him than she let on. Maybe she was testing him, seeing if he would tell her the truth. "I don't know where she is. The last time I saw her was in Shades Harbor."

"Ooh, so he lured you out of the ghost village but left your sister behind," said Grannie Yaga. "That's interesting, that is."

"Who lured me? Are you talking about the Piper?"

"Yes," she said, clapping her hands together. "Grannie's question again."

"Wait," said Carter. "I didn't mean—"

"*My* question," she said, and this time there was a dangerous edge to her tone. Carter shut his mouth and waited. Better to let her ask him another question than to make her angry, he supposed. He didn't know what she had planned for him, but whatever it was, stalling seemed to be a good idea.

"Grannie's question is, would you like to hear a story?" she asked.

Carter wasn't sure he'd heard her right. That was not a question he'd been expecting. "A story? Yeah, okay. I guess."

"Good. This story is known by many names, but Grannie calls it 'The Two Magicians.'" Grannie Yaga rocked in her chair, grinning. "It is a grand and proper tale, so I'll speaks it proper for you now:

Once upon a time, an old peddler and a young piper sailed together across the great Sea of Troubles. For long days and nights, they tossed about on that lonely ocean. Some days the wind refused to blow and the water was as still as glass, and when they stared at it, all their worries were reflected back at them. At night, terrible storms would threaten to tear their boat to pieces and drown them both. But during the day, the piper played music to keep their spirits up. And when their boat was battered about in the storms, the peddler tied himself and the piper together with such strong bonds that neither fell overboard.

After many months of hardship, just when they thought the Sea of Troubles would finally swallow them whole, the peddler spotted a lone, distant island. Though the ship was nearly falling apart beneath their feet, they raised the sail, and when the wind gave out, they paddled with their hands, and when the ship itself gave out, they swam. Though they very nearly drowned, the two washed up on the new shore and found there a great green country.

The air was warm and the sun shined most every day, and the nights never grew all the way dark. The peddler set out at once to map their new island home, and in his travels he discovered a magnificent road that stretched from one shore to the other.

For a time, the young piper traveled with the peddler, and the peddler revealed himself to be a great magician, and taught the piper the ways of magic. They befriended an elf princess in a deep forest, and they traded with the kobolds. But though the piper had traveled far from the sea, when he was quiet, he could still hear the waves and he could not forget the vast and terrible waters he'd sailed.

A sadness overtook the lad, and he left the peddler's side and drifted alone into dark places. There he found the shunned creatures, the witches, the demons and the monsters that hid in the dark, and these beasts taught the piper many lessons he had never before learned. But he played music to soothe their hateful souls, and in return, they gifted him a magic pipe that made him a powerful magician himself.

Ages passed, and the peddler still walked his road and was content. But the piper never forgot his sadness, and he was much changed. He carried his demons with him wherever he went, and he set his monsters loose on any that angered him. He grew spiteful and jealous of others' happiness.

This caused a terrible battle between the two magicians, between master and apprentice. The piper and the peddler met on the field of battle, and though the piper had grown strong, the elf princess lent her power to the peddler, and the piper was defeated. As punishment, they took his magic pipe and locked him away in a black tower where no one would find him.

The piper was defeated, but it had come at a cost. Though the Sea of Troubles was long gone, it left new troubles in its wake:

To the piper was left the trouble of Vengeance Denied.

To the peddler was left the dual troubles of Responsibility and Regret.

And the magical land began to darken, and all was not well.

"And that," said Grannie Yaga, "is all Grannie knows of the tale, though it's not, I suspects, the end. *He* hates it when anyone tells this particular story, and there's few these days who will dare, so you consider this a gift from your Grannie Yaga."

The old witch leaned forward in her chair. "You see, it's like the story says—some troubles can't never be forgotten, and woe be to them that try."

Carter watched the old hag rock back and forth. His father told stories. Carter told stories, and he knew well how stories were often true without being factual. Truth got to the heart of something, like a problem or a feeling, even if the tales one told to explain that truth were all made up. It was true that you shouldn't stop to talk to a stranger in the woods, even if that stranger wasn't really a wolf.

Grannie Yaga's story had the ring of truth to it. The piper of the story had to be the Pied Piper of Hamelin. The peddler was the same mysterious person who'd made Lukas's map, and it was his road they'd been following. And Emilie had mentioned that the elves had a princess who never left her castle. So these three were connected in some way, and what's more, they'd been friends. But what was fact and what was true?

"That was a good story, Grannie Yaga," said Carter.

"What a proper, sweet boy you are," she answered.

"But now I get to ask a question, because I think we skipped my turn."

Grannie Yaga leaned forward in her chair. "I'm not sure I wants to keep playing."

"Just one more," said Carter, eyeing the old witch warily. "My question is, are you going to let me go?"

"Go where? Should I let you loose in the Bonewood?"

"If, maybe, you could point me in the direction of the Peddler's Road . . ."

"The Peddler's Road?" Grannie Yaga rose up out of her chair. "Didn't Grannie's story teach you anything? That magician is an idiot. Grannie and the Peddler have a history, a long history. Today he walks that nasty road of his, keeping my lovely forest boxed in, won't let it grow. Course, you know there's a whole village of tender young children like yourself just across the river, but the Peddler won't let Grannie anywhere near them." Grannie Yaga leaned forward on her cudgel and smiled, showing every last one of her hideous wooden teeth. "And once upon a time that old rascal stole Grannie's magic map and the prophecy that went with it, did you know that? Cheated her in trade, he did. But Grannie will have her revenge, yes she will. Soon. Very soon."

Carter felt the color drain from his cheeks. Lukas told them that the Peddler had gotten the map from a witch in the woods. Grannie Yaga must've been that witch, which meant that the prophecy was also hers. Had they been following a lie?

Grannie Yaga snatched up her sack from the table and held it over her simmering cauldron. From where he was standing, Carter couldn't see the contents as she emptied them into the pot, but the underside of the bag had soaked through with something wet and fearful-looking. The witch muttered over her brew, and it began to shimmer with an unhealthful greenish glow.

"I knows you can hear me," she said, staring into her pot. "I told you to trust your Grannie, and now what I saw is coming to pass. The boy is here with me. What will you give me for him?"

Nothing answered, at least nothing that Carter could hear, but Grannie Yaga grinned and nodded. "Done," she said. "I suppose we'll come to you, seeing as you're not going anywheres! Don't worry, we'll be there quicker than a dead man's sigh."

The light faded from the cauldron, and Grannie Yaga took up her stout cudgel and whacked it against her iron pot three times. It clanged loudly in Carter's ears, but before the ringing had stopped, he detected another sound, a low groan like creaking wood. Then the floor beneath him started to tilt, and Carter had to throw out his hands to keep from falling over. He grabbed hold of the window bars for balance, and as he looked outside, he saw that their little hut was actually rising up off the forest floor, standing tall on two enormous legs.

"To answer your last question, boy," said Grannie Yaga.

"I am not letting you go. There's someone special wants to see you, and he's been waiting a long, long time."

The hut swayed precariously, and jars and pots began sliding across the table. Bandybulb rolled about helplessly in his cage as Grannie Yaga's hut began walking through the forest.

"Better take a seat," said the old witch, cackling again. "It can be a bumpy ride!"

CHAPTER THIRTY

"Why would he go in there?" Max was asking. "Why on earth would my brother wander off into such a terrible place?"

Lukas didn't have an answer. If only he knew, if only *any* of them knew what had driven Carter into that horrible forest. There was sorcery at work here, and whatever dark power had pitted itself against them, it wanted Carter most of all.

Lukas cursed himself for a fool. He had promised Max that he'd look after her brother, and while he'd been asleep, for the few hours each night that Lukas let his guard down, Carter had been kidnapped. Lukas had failed. Leon wouldn't have failed. An Eldest Boy deserving of the title would have found a way to keep Carter safe, even against an enemy that haunted their dreams.

But this wasn't a time for self-pity. Lukas was sure that

Carter hadn't run away of his own volition. Though they were following only one set of tracks, Lukas suspected that poor Carter hadn't been alone, not really. Something was pulling him along, drawing him near until . . .

The boy's tracks ended at a wide creek bridged by the Peddler's Road. It might have been a pretty spot once, but the creek now belonged to the Bonewood. The spread of that evil forest had reached this far, and the underbrush of twisting vines and thornbushes stretched out onto the Peddler's Road as if seeking to strangle it, to choke it until there was no road left—just Bonewood. But the road endured still, and the forest could spread no farther. The bridge was derelict, and crumbling in places as the unwholesome vegetation worked its way into the cracks and seams, slowly pulling it apart. The creek beneath was filled with murky, noxious water. It looked deeper and more menacing than any creek had a right to be, and yet it was here that Carter had left the road.

Lukas studied the trees, looking for any sign of the boy's passing, while Paul stared worriedly down at the black creek water. Lukas knew what the scout was thinking, although he would not speak his fear out loud. If Carter had fallen in there, they'd never know it. Lukas tried not to imagine what might be living in there.

"Can you track him?" asked Lukas.

"I can try," said Paul. "But the Bonewood isn't like other forests. It will work against you. Cover up tracks and mislead you on purpose."

"What are you saying?" asked Max. "Are you saying these woods are alive?"

"All woods are alive," said Paul. "This one's just meaner than most."

Their quest was falling apart around them. Lukas had barely been able to look Max in the eye ever since they'd discovered Carter was missing. Her brother was brave, as brave as anyone Lukas knew, but bravery was rarely enough when you were alone in the wild.

"All right, then," said Lukas, drawing his dagger. "If Carter went into the Bonewood, that's where we go, too." He turned to Max. "I won't bother asking you to wait here."

"You'd have to tie me up first," she said.

Lukas had lost his rope back at the troll bridge, or else he would have considered it. Out there in the Bonewood, it would be hard enough searching for Carter without having to keep an eye on Max as well. It was said that a witch hunted in those trees and ogres roamed about, squashing anyone they happened upon. Max wasn't behaving rationally—one look at her ruined feet was proof of that. But then, Lukas wondered what he would do if the person he cared for most suddenly went missing.

They hadn't taken more than a few steps off the road when they heard the sounds of something approaching. They were distant noises at first, like something huge stomping through the forest. Whatever it was, it was getting closer.

"Ogres?" asked Lukas, eyeing the trees.

"Maybe," Paul answered. "Hope not."

Lukas held his dagger in front of him, as if the small blade would do any good against something that could make that much noise. "Everyone hide!" Lukas said. "Find cover!"

But it was too late. From the trees came bursting a sight that might have been comical under different circumstances. A rickety old hut on top of a pair of enormous clawed chicken legs. Bone wind chimes dangled from the hut and made a sound like a children's rattle as the shack swayed back and forth on its spindly legs.

The hut creature reared backward as it "saw" Lukas and his friends scrambling for cover, and from within came a horrible shrieking laughter. "Ooh, what's down there?" cried the voice. "Morsels for Grannie? Be a nice boy and fetch Grannie her good teeth, would you dear?"

Lukas managed to jump out of the way just in time to avoid the grasping talons of one of the hut's feet. As he rolled to standing, he swung and stabbed at the creature's toe, but his dagger merely bounced off the thick skin.

"Run!" Emilie was shouting, but there was another voice calling to them as well. An impossible voice.

Lukas looked up. There in the hut's window was Carter, his face pressed against the iron bars. "Max!" Carter shouted. "Lukas! I'm up here!"

Max had heard him, too, but in her panic to get to her brother, she was rushing forward, heedless of the clawed foot that was rising again, preparing to strike.

"Ha-ha," cackled the mysterious voice. "Maybe I'll squash them into jelly, eh, sweet boy? Jam for our toast!"

"No!" Carter shouted at their unseen enemy. "Don't hurt them!"

But whatever was controlling that hut wasn't listening to Carter. The foot rose up over Max, ready to stomp her flat.

Lukas dove forward and tackled Max, knocking both of

them out of the foot's path. Then they tumbled, one over the other, off the road and through the underbrush, toward the creek. Max's cloak got caught on a bramble bush and arrested her fall, while Lukas kept on rolling right into the creek, into the black water.

The cold hit him like a winter gale. His first thought was, *How could water in the summer get so cold?* An unnatural numbness began to spread along his hands and feet as he sank farther. It was dark under there, dark and frigid.

Lukas twisted around, but which way was up? He kicked, but he was tangled in his own cloak, and he'd never been a very good swimmer. This was his nightmare come to life. Panic gripped him. He needed to breathe.

Then he saw a shape making its way toward him through the cloudy water. A rescuer, perhaps. As it drew near, he saw long, bony fingers and a beard like seaweed, sprouting from an old man's twisted face. Not a rescuer, then. It was reaching for him, and Lukas was going to die.

Then the creature turned and vanished, quickly fleeing to whatever shadowy depths it called home. Something else bumped Lukas in the back of the head, and he saw a branch being lowered into the water. Lukas grabbed hold as the branch began to lift, and Lukas rode it up, up, up.

He broke the surface with a choking gasp, and at last he could breathe. Arms reached for him, and he allowed himself to be dragged out of the vile creek and onto shore. He was shivering from the chill that had settled in his bones.

Max was next to him, wrapping her own dry cloak around him and holding him close so that her own warmth might add to his.

"I almost didn't remember," she said, looking down at Lukas with relief.

"R-remember what?" he said, and he coughed up a mouthful of black water.

"Nokk, nokk, nokk," she said.

"Who's there?" he answered weakly.

"I can't believe it worked," she said. "When I saw that thing reaching for you, I wasn't sure it would. Where did it come from?"

"The dark," answered Lukas, then pulled himself up to sitting and looked around. The hut was gone, and Paul and Emilie were standing over him with looks of intense worry.

"Where's Carter?" he said.

"That hut thing ran away, and it took him with it," said Max, quietly.

"What happened?"

Emilie and Paul exchanged a queer look, and Paul pointed back up the hill to the road. "He happened," the boy said.

Standing on the road was an ugly little man wearing a backpack twice as big as he was. It was comically stuffed with objects; a lute with its strings missing, a birdcage with a bird missing, a dented crown and a shovel shaped like a hand were just a few of the odd items that Lukas could see poking out. The little man looked at Lukas and scowled, spitting over his shoulder as he did so.

"Idiot children," he muttered.

They'd found the Peddler at last.

❧ CHAPTER THIRTY-ONE ❧

The Peddler turned out to be just about the ugliest man Max had ever seen. It wasn't so much that he was physically ugly, though he was that—hunchbacked, with a few stray whiskers that could not rightly be called a beard and a bumpy face stitched together with wrinkles. No, it was more that the Peddler *acted* ugly. He spat and cussed at the little fire that he was trying to build on the side of the road, and every now and then he'd glare up at Max and her friends, standing several yards away for safety, and shake his head disapprovingly.

Max elbowed Lukas in the ribs. "He's not what I was expecting."

"You'll get used to him."

"Really?" said Paul. "Well, she'd be the first."

"I think we should ask for his help," said Lukas.

"What sort of help?" asked Max. "He doesn't exactly seem friendly."

Lukas leaned close. "He may not look impressive—"

"Or smell impressive," interrupted Paul.

"But he *is* a magician," continued Lukas. "And he might be able to help us find Carter."

"Might as well stop your whispering and gawking," called the Peddler. "Come close and tell me what you're doing on my road."

Max followed Lukas as they joined the Peddler next to his little fire. The little man was now tending to a cast-iron skillet filled with plump, sizzling sausages, the smell of which made Max's mouth water so that she had to remind her stomach that she didn't eat meat.

The Peddler uncorked a clay jug and poured some kind of thick syrup over the frying sausages. Then he speared a sausage with a bent fork he'd produced from inside his pack and lifted it to his mouth, dripping grease and syrup all down his chin and beard. Max noticed that he pointedly didn't offer to share.

"We're glad to see you, Peddler," said Lukas.

"Course you are," said the Peddler, through a mouthful. "If I hadn't wandered along, you all would be just so much mush squished between giant chicken toes. Whatever are you New Hameliners doing so far from home, anyway?"

Although he seemed to be speaking to them as a group, Max noticed that the Peddler was staring directly at her. Maybe he'd never seen a girl with pink hair, either, but Max didn't care. Nothing else mattered so long as Carter was in trouble.

"That thing took my little brother," said Max.

"Brother?" grumbled the Peddler.

"His name is Carter," said Lukas. "We spotted him in the window of whatever that creature was."

"Was he baked in a pie?"

"No!" said Max.

"That's good," said the Peddler. "That *thing* you all keep talking about is Grannie Yaga's enchanted hut—Grannie Yaga being a particularly vicious sort of witch. I say it's good because if Grannie Yaga was going to eat your friend, she would've cooked him by now."

"Cooked him?" Max felt Lukas's hand on her arm, but she shrugged it off.

"At least she doesn't eat them raw," said the Peddler matter-of-factly.

Max stomped her bandaged feet, the simple act of which felt like she was jumping on thorns. "We have to follow them. We have to get my brother back!"

"You won't catch up with her," said the Peddler. "Not on foot and not by yourselves, you won't."

"Please, Peddler," said Lukas. "Then how do we get him back?"

"That depends on where she's taking him."

"Where?" said Max. "Do you know?"

The Peddler squinted one eye up at her. "Well, I have an idea where she might be headed, but it depends on who your brother is—and who you are, for that matter. By your hair and your clothes you're obviously not from New Hamelin, and you're not a ghost. Not sure I should care either way, but since we're talking . . ."

Max suddenly had the strong urge to snatch the Peddler's